LX1

"I'm going to kiss you soon..."

Gray's words were a statement of intent and not a request. Laney's body sure noticed the difference. Gray wasn't taking her anywhere. Not only was he bossy and domineering, but he *knew* it and he wasn't making any excuses for it. She shouldn't have been so turned on by it, but...she was.

Oh, God. Was she ever. With Gray, she wouldn't have to give directions or look after her own orgasm. He was dangerous.

She sucked in a breath and angled a little bit closer, until her thighs bumped against his. She could *do* this. Be sexy and bold and fun. "How about now?"

"I can do that." His thumb stroked over her lower lip. Good, she decided. But not enough.

She fisted the front of his T-shirt, inching him closer. "Do it."

Before I lose my courage.

He grinned.

"Your wish is my command..."

D0048706

Dear Reader,

Fantasies are one of my favorite things to explore. Part of that, of course, is me daydreaming (even if my husband isn't convinced that staring out the window is a valuable research tool). Everyone has fantasies—it's just that some of us don't find it easy to ask for what we want, particularly in bed. But...what if there *was* an easier way to whisper a fantasy to a lover? A sexy, fun and flirty way?

When Laney Parker visits Fantasy Island, a very exclusive private Caribbean island resort, she learns that the resort's guests have a shorthand code for sharing their sexual fantasies. The resort's cocktail menu is a list of sexy drink names—choose a drink and you choose your fantasy. *Sex on the Beach*, *All Night Long*, *Between the Sheets*, *Blue Negligee*. Some names are raunchy; some are sweeter and less blush-inducing (if no less fun). When Laney meets Gray Jackson, our hero, she suddenly sees the appeal of picking a fantasy from a menu because there are all sorts of things she'd like to try with him.

As a trauma surgeon, Laney is used to being in control of every facet of her life. She's disciplined, mentally strong and good at giving orders. What she doesn't know is how to let go. Gray Jackson, the leader of the undercover SEAL team that has infiltrated Fantasy Island in order to take down a dangerous drug lord, is just the man to tease her into giving up some of that control. He has a few fantasies of his own, and soon he and Laney are burning up the sheets together.

I hope you enjoy their story. If you want to chat with me about this or other books, you can find me on Twitter and Facebook.

Happy reading!

Anne Marsh

Anne Marsh

Teasing Her SEAL

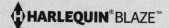

If you purchased this book without a cover you should be aware that this book is stolen property. It was reported as "unsold and destroyed" to the publisher, and neither the author nor the publisher has received any payment for this "stripped book."

Recycling programs
for this product may
not exist in your area.

ISBN-13: 978-0-373-79867-4

Teasing Her SEAL

Copyright © 2015 by Anne Marsh

All rights reserved. Except for use in any review, the reproduction or utilization of this work in whole or in part in any form by any electronic, mechanical or other means, now known or hereinafter invented, including xerography, photocopying and recording, or in any information storage or retrieval system, is forbidden without the written permission of the publisher, Harlequin Enterprises Limited, 225 Duncan Mill Road, Don Mills, Ontario M3B 3K9, Canada.

This is a work of fiction. Names, characters, places and incidents are either the product of the author's imagination or are used fictitiously, and any resemblance to actual persons, living or dead, business establishments, events or locales is entirely coincidental.

This edition published by arrangement with Harlequin Books S.A.

For questions and comments about the quality of this book, please contact us at CustomerService@Harlequin.com.

® and TM are trademarks of Harlequin Enterprises Limited or its corporate affiliates. Trademarks indicated with ® are registered in the United States Patent and Trademark Office, the Canadian Intellectual Property Office and in other countries.

Printed in U.S.A.

www.Harlequin.com

Anne Marsh writes sexy contemporary and paranormal romances because the world can always enjoy one more alpha male. She started writing romance after getting laid off from her job as a technical writer—and quickly decided happily-ever-afters trumped software manuals. She lives in Northern California with her family and six cats.

Books by Anne Marsh

HARLEQUIN BLAZE

Wicked Sexy
Wicked Nights
Wicked Secrets

To get the inside scoop on Harlequin Blaze and its talented writers, be sure to check out BlazeAuthors.com.

All backlist available in ebook format.

Visit the Author Profile page at Harlequin.com for more titles.

This one's for Gwen Hayes. Honestly, all books should be for her because she rocks. Awesome writer. Amazing editor. Hilarious Tweet-er, thinker-upper of sekkrit book projects and exercise *raconteur*. Thanks for sharing the writing journey with me.

1

"HUNGRY?" THE DANCER gyrating in front of Lieutenant Commander Gray Jackson's table wasn't pushing burgers or chicken wings. She ran a hand down her body, highlighting various edible spots. Her costume—or lack thereof, because she rocked a barely there thong and a pair of four-inch Lucite heels—offered plenty to look at. It was a sad commentary on the state of Gray's sex life, however, that the skin show left him unmoved, without so much as a twitch from the boys.

"Darling, I'm always ready to eat." He ponied up the teasing words automatically, because his cover as a bad-boy biker required acting like a jerk. When he didn't follow up with a cash offer, the blonde pouted and moved on to the next table. Too bad, so sad.

The Born To Ride was a seedy dive bar popular with motorcycle gangs. On a mission to infiltrate the outlaw biker gang M-Breed and shut down their arms pipeline, Gray's squad had been deep undercover as potential recruits for the past six months. It was a scene Gray recognized all too well from his wilder, younger years. Dancers shimmied up and down poles on a raised platform to the banging pulse of the music, while the patrons knocked back beers and shots, broken up by the occasional bar fight or game of pool. This was *not* the kind of place a man took a date. The men here were interested in three things: drinking, drugs and dealing. Sex, when it happened, was quick, rough and accomplished in the alley or the bathroom stall. They were also, by and large, ex-military and patch-wearing members of M-Breed.

Gray fit right in, and only partly because he'd grown up tough and fighting. He'd ridden from an early age, joining a local biker gang with his cousins and chewing up the highway whenever he could fill a tank. He'd done more than his fair share of juvenile law-breaking and, if he hadn't enlisted in the US Navy when one of his cousins had, he'd have most likely ended up here, anyhow. Instead, he was a SEAL and active-duty military. If tonight's mission went well, they'd finally have M-Breed's lieutenants selling arms on tape. Lights out, show over, go directly to federal prison and serve ten to twenty. Both of the guys at Gray's table tonight were members of his team. Levi Brandon and Mason Black had his back and his six. Outside and down the street, Sam Nale and Remy Leveaux worked the tech detail, monitoring the wires Gray, Levi and Mason wore.

A fistfight broke out in a far corner of the bar, but the ruckus barely merited a second glance. If trouble headed in Gray's direction, the Glock tucked in his waistband had him covered. And, when he ran out of bullets, he had a pair of knives down his motorcycle boots and a length of chain in his jacket pocket. Add to that his two hands, and he didn't need more to kick ass in a fight. God, he hoped there was a fight tonight. He had energy to burn and then some. Fight for Uncle Sam, bust some heads in the names of freedom and democracy. He loved his job.

"Aww, I think you broke her heart," Levi drawled, eyeing the dancer's butt as she worked a new table.

"That's the way it goes."

Levi flipped Gray the bird, but the man was grinning, so his tender feelings were just fine. Unlike Gray. He had no idea when his sex drive had hung a left and disappeared, but casual sex left him cold now. The empty beer bottles lined up in front of him were as much window-dressing as the interest he'd briefly feigned in the female shimmying and shaking her way over to him. Which was kind of a shame. Two years ago he'd have enjoyed the attention, but now he was dead inside.

Mason tapped the table. "Company manners, boys. Our date just walked in the front door. He's not a pretty bitch, but then, neither are we."

Gray checked out the door and, sure enough, it was showtime. Spokes, M-Breed's second lieutenant, saun-tered toward the bar, towing a petite blonde in his wake. The blonde was his old lady and Friday-night bar ac-cessory, although how a crusty fifty-year-old man like Spokes had scored this fetching twentysomething was debatable. Cash or drugs—Gray would have laid money on one or both as the culprits. Spokes had gotten his name after stabbing a guy with a handful of motorcycle spokes in a chop shop. He'd done five years on a man-slaughter rap before rejoining the gang. He was a mean bastard who preferred fists to words, as the rainbow of bruises on his old lady's arms attested.

Emily. Her name was Emily. Gray would damn well use her name, rather than the label that marked her as belonging to Spokes.

Spokes might not be parting with Emily, but he had agreed to sell Gray a trunkload of high-caliber automatic weaponry for bargain-basement pricing. AK-47s weren't the kind of firearms that should be available on the street, although Spokes clearly didn't give a crap about where his guns ended up.

"You want me to see if I can detach Spokes's arm candy?"

The fourth member of Gray's undercover team, Ashley Dixon, wasn't actually a SEAL—since the SEALs had yet to induct a female member. She'd been borrowed from the DEA to provide mission-critical cover, pretending to be Levi's girlfriend. She perched on the man's knee as if he were a chair, a skintight minidress skimming the tops of her thighs.

Gray's phone vibrated before he could answer Ashley, and he automatically pulled it out, checking the screen. Around him, Levi and Mason did the same. Yeah. From the disbelieving looks on their faces, he knew their phones were also flashing the code word to pull out. What. The. Hell?

"You seeing what I'm seeing?" Maybe the alcohol fumes had finally done a number on his brain.

Levi nodded, looking pissed off. "We need to roll."

Fine. He'd fall back, but first he had a detour to make. "Detach Spokes's girlfriend. Get her out on the dance floor."

Ashley slid off Levi's lap. "I've got this."

Busy pounding tequila shots, Spokes didn't object when Ashley tugged the man's lady out onto the dance floor. Ashley bumped and spun, the hem of her cocktail dress inching its way up her muscled thighs. She dipped and worked her hips in an exaggerated shimmy, and her companion flashed a smile and followed suit. Ashley looked happy, and Gray didn't think it was an act. She enjoyed dancing and so she was seizing the moment. The awkward bump of her butt against her companion's had them both laughing.

Levi watched the pair, a frown on his face. "Where do you think she learned to dance like that?"

"Not at Saturday ballet class." She demonstrated a serious lack of rhythm and finesse, but her enthusiasm was contagious. Ashley had a life outside the DEA and her undercover work. He, on the other hand, was a SEAL. End of story. If he ever walked away from his team, he was nothing. A big, blank page of nothing. He didn't have any family he'd stayed in contact with, which he could only partially blame on his work for the government. Sure, he couldn't share the details—or anything much at all—about the covert missions, but he also hadn't tried.

Since his inner shrink had apparently decided to work overtime, he could admit that he was hollow inside, carting around a crater-sized hole that couldn't be filled by gunfights or the adrenaline rush of nailing a dangerous assignment. He'd tried the bar scene and the fight clubs, but the alcohol left him with a hangover, and the fight clubs gave him two broken ribs. Neither were long-term options, and at least he'd been smart enough to recognize that truth. Now he ran on empty. No love, no faith in anything but his guns and his guys, nothing to look forward to but the next time he shipped out and the next firefight.

Speaking of which, it was time to get this show on the road. Shoving to his feet, he headed toward the dance floor. His guys fell in behind him, ready to hump their asses onto a plane, fly down to Central America and take care of whatever it was that needed doing there. They were real fucking Musketeers, and that was the truth. They'd have his back, even on the dance floor, where way too many bodies did the bump and grind. Some of the dancers were pretty, others were not. He knew which category he fell into, although his face didn't stop hands and thighs from touching him in a way that was pure invitation. He was big. He had money. And in the world of the motorcycle gang, that put him at the top of the food chain until someone else knocked him down.

"Ladies." He inclined his head as he joined the dancing duo, and Ashley pulled him into her circle of two. Spokes's girlfriend gave him a quick once-over, looking nervous, and darted a glance over her shoulder. Spokes must not have protested, because she stayed put. They danced silently for a moment, the music pulsing around them and vibrating through the soles of his boots, and he almost got why Ashley liked this.

The bruises on the blonde's arms, however, were even more disturbing close-up. His own relationships might not last longer than a night, and he might need his sex raw and gritty, but hurting his partner was off-limits. No exceptions. Whether or not the US Government had enough to put the scumbag away for a few decades, the lady needed a breather. Unfortunately, while her tired eyes flitted between him and the man waiting for her at the bar, she showed no signs of heading for the door.

He put his mouth right up by her ear, making sure she had no excuse to not hear him over the pounding beat of the bar music. "Emily, you need to pick up and get the hell away from Spokes."

Maybe she tweaked or maybe Spokes's cash spoke

louder than the man's charming personality. Either way, breaking Spokes's nose wouldn't get her to the door if she didn't want to leave. A woman had to want to walk, and she also had to be ready. He'd learned that first-hand when he'd been six. The trailer park where he'd grown up hadn't been big on personal space or privacy. When a man and a woman fought, the neighbors heard every word, every grunt, every slap of flesh on flesh. He slipped Emily a wad of cash. Money wasn't enough, but it was a start. She'd have to do the rest of the work herself. After a moment, she nodded and laid in a new course for the side door. With the cash, she'd have a chance, but only if she kept on walking and didn't return home where Spokes could find her.

Still, it was hard to turn away, towing Ashley with him as if he'd busted up the dance circle simply to collect her. It helped some that all hell broke loose behind them as two of the bar's patrons got into a fistfight that rapidly escalated to criminal property damage and felony assault and battery. He'd given up pretending that he minded the violence. Because truth was, violence came with the territory, and his team had ended more than one mission that way.

The Harleys he and his boys had parked outside were, hands down, the best perk of this particular mission, especially since it looked as if they wouldn't be taking Spokes down any other way tonight. Ashley had complained loud and long that she hadn't scored a bike of her own, but an independent ride didn't fit the biker girlfriend image.

Mason turned the ignition switch on and shifted his bike into neutral. "Where we headed?"

Gray rechecked his phone. "I've got one word for you. *Belize*."

"What's in Belize?" Levi kicked the starter hard, his bike firing to life.

It was a good question. Up until five minutes ago, Gray would have answered jungle, scrubland, historic ruins and some damned good fly-fishing. He might even have fantasized once or twice about buying a piece of land on one of those little sandy cays and putting up a house. Sitting out in all that blue, casting a line. He sighed. Whatever undercover op Uncle Sam needed them for now, it sure wouldn't involve a cold one and a fishing lure.

"Our next op. We're going undercover as resort staff at some place called Fantasy Island." He gunned the bike toward the highway. Another night, another mission, even if this one came with blue water and palm trees. Yeah. The odds of him passing as the employee of a five-star resort seemed low, but he went where he was sent, and he'd do what it took to get the job done. He'd never blown his cover yet.

Hooyah.

THE SEAPLANE LURCHED, and Laney Parker dug her nails out of her armrest. When she risked a glance out the window, she spotted nothing but Caribbean blue beneath them, the ocean's flat surface dotted with shadows from the clouds. The view was pretty, but missing any kind of landing zone whatsoever. She'd triaged a small plane crash her first year in the UCSF emergency room, and the injuries had been particularly horrific.

The plane bounced again, and she immediately re-attached herself to the armrest. Although the odds of dying in a plane crash were low, it hadn't been her week for playing the odds. Her stomach rose halfway up her throat. She'd pass on the meet-and-greet with the ocean's surface. Leaning forward, she riffled through the seat pocket contents. The charter airline had stocked up on glossy magazines, but skimped on the barf bags. For the ridiculous price tag this week in the tropics had cost, she'd use the magazines if she had to. What was supposed to be a week of glamorous sex with her new husband by her side was most definitely *not* turning out as planned. Still, when the plane leveled out, she exhaled slowly. Maybe surviving the landing was in the cards, after all.

The sound of a cork popping and champagne fizzing had her head turning in time to catch the flash of a long-necked bottle out of the corner of her eye. Frankly, she wasn't sure how anyone could think of drinking so early in the morning—although it was definitely five o'clock somewhere. The woman who dropped into the seat opposite her, however, didn't look as if she cared about what the rest of the world thought. Ever. It was a good look, and one Laney needed to emulate. *Screw it*. That was her new motto, and she'd buy the T-shirt just as soon as she could.

Maybe Fantasy Island had a gift shop.

The woman had ink-black hair and an ear full of piercings that must have given the TSA fits. She'd paired the metal-head look with jeans, a ripped concert T-shirt from a band Laney had never heard of and a pair of military-issue combat boots. An audible, fist-pumping beat issued from her earbuds. Laney, on the other hand, sported her usual yoga wear from Target in practical black. Dark colors didn't show the blood, and since as a trauma surgeon, she tended to get called in whenever she wasn't actually already *at* the hospital, there was no point in not being comfortable or racking up a dry cleaning bill. In fact, now that she thought about it, her yoga pants were just about the only thing she owned that weren't hospital-blue or wedding-white.

Right. *So* not going there.

Champagne dripped onto the carpet as her new seatmate brandished a trio of flutes. Amusement sparkled in her eyes as she popped the earbuds out.

"Want some?"

Ten o'clock in the morning, Laney's brain volunteered. *Wouldn't be prudent.* Sure, partaking would be fun, but the careful habits of a lifetime were awfully hard to break.

Her hostess jiggled the bottle. "It's free."

Nothing was free. As Laney's credit card company had called to remind her yesterday.

"You look as if you could use a drink." Goth Princess leaned forward, revealing that she'd skipped a bra that morning. When she reached over to offer a flute to the third woman in the cabin, she followed the boob shoot with a flash of neon-green thong, which was way more than Laney needed to know about the woman's preferences in the underwear department.

"I'm good," she said.

Which was part of the problem, wasn't it?

When Laney didn't take the flute, the other woman curled up in her seat and grinned. "Two for me. Yay."

"If we're experiencing turbulence, you should probably buckle up." PSA…achieved.

Goth Princess shrugged and knocked back half the flute. "What's the worst that can happen?"

Laney knew exactly what could happen. "Fractures, head trauma, a snapped spine—all are likely outcomes of a hard-impact crash landing. If we hit something besides water, add road rash and possible burns to the list."

"Wow." Goth Princess nodded but didn't lose her death grip on the bottle. Instead, she propped the buckle against her stomach, ramming the clasp in with her elbow. "Good points."

Message received. Safety *and* champagne were an option. "Actually, I've changed my mind..."

Reaching over, Laney snagged the second flute. She was probably performing a second public service because she had no doubts whatsoever that Goth Princess would drink both. And, since the other woman clearly weighed some minuscule, waifish amount—unlike Laney—she'd be drunk before the seaplane ever landed. Or crashed. Whichever came first. Laney swallowed a sip of champagne reflexively. She should have been a married woman by now, but her fiancé had kicked the week off by cheating on her. On day two, she'd negotiated with the wedding venues—and been forcibly reminded of the meaning of *nonrefundable deposit*. On day three, her credit card company had called to not-so-gently remind her that they appreciated prompt payments, and her upcoming vacation to Fantasy Island had overextended her credit limit. Day four? No more job.

Not working double shifts in the trauma bay should have allowed her to finally catch up on her sleep, but her head wouldn't stop running options to address days one, two and three. She hadn't even processed the unfairness of being the one who had to give up her job because her fiancé had been caught having sex at work with another woman—and her continued presence at the hospital would make *him* feel uncomfortable—because that needed to happen on a beach while clutching a Mai Tai. Plus, since even God had rested on the seventh day, she was really hoping today would go better.

"So." The cabin's only other occupant leaned around her seat to take them both in. Laney had no idea where the redhead had found a pink suit, but instead of screaming *board of trustees* or *clash worthy of a circus clown*, the cinched-in jacket with a ruffle promised fun and sassy. Or maybe that was the spray of freckles covering the woman's nose. "Spill. What are you doing here?"

"I'm on my honeymoon."

She swigged more champagne. Huh. Somehow, she'd reached the bottom of the glass, which didn't even have the decency to be half-full. Goth Princess leaned forward and obligingly topped her off, temporarily fixing the problem.

Pink Suit blinked and eyeballed the cabin. The three of them were the only passengers. "Lose someone?"

That was one way to put it.

"He decided getting married wasn't in his plans. Since our tickets to Fantasy Island were nonrefundable *and* he preceded his antimarriage announcement in front of the entire surgical unit with cheating on me, here I am. Laney Parker, MD. Unemployed, newly single and extremely broke."

The movers had taken her pitifully few boxes from his condo straight to storage. She'd deal with permanent relocation when she got back.

"That's harsh." Goth Princess stuck her free hand out. "I'm Ashley Dixon. I won a free ticket. Sorry."

Laney shook the woman's hand, the plane promptly lurched and champagne went everywhere. Hell. Wiping her palm on the superexpensive leather seats was probably a social faux pas, but it was that or her twelve-dollar yoga pants. Ashley licked her champagne-covered fingers. "Even better than spitting and swearing to be blood sisters."

"Gross." Pink Suit extended her own hand, displaying a really pretty French manicure, but no rings. "Madeline Holmes. I write a wedding blog."

Free ticket. Gainfully employed. Yep. Laney had definitely drawn the short straw.

"I need snacks." The champagne suddenly hit her empty stomach like a Mack truck barreling into a freeway retaining wall, the results of which she'd seen firsthand last week and which were decidedly unpleasant. She unbuckled and stood up. Never mind the possibility of blunt trauma injuries in the immediate future—she needed something salty. *Now.* Madeline grinned. "What happened to snapped spines and bashed-in heads?"

"I'm hungry. And really bad turbulence would bounce you hard enough in your seat to fracture your spine, anyhow. Or you'd slam your head back into the headrest."

Ashley blinked. "Wow. Thanks for the visual."

"You try working six days a week in a trauma bay in San Francisco." She'd stopped sugarcoating approximately three hours into her first day on the job. She walked down the narrow aisle toward what looked like a small galley. Beneath the elegant granite counter was a stainless-steel fridge. She yanked open the door, leaving behind a sticky smear of champagne, and hit the mother lode. The seaplane folks had stashed an entire tray of chocolate-covered strawberries inside the fridge. Something salty would have been better, but who could pass up chocolate fruit? Plus, maybe if she ate her weight in treats, she'd feel better about the credit card bill.

"What kind of doctor?" Madeline asked at the same moment that Ashley yelled "Share!"

"Trauma surgeon." Gunshot wounds, stabbings, freeway car pile-ups…she had seen plenty of action.

Her cases were unlike the small regional hospital in the Midwest where her mother worked, or the slightly larger, but not much busier hospital in Stockton, California, that had an unexpected need for a good ER surgeon. Of course, her mother had also come through for her, and she appreciated the offer letter tucked in the bottom of her bag. Really. All she had to do was sign on the dotted line and she'd be gainfully employed again. In the middle of nowhere.

She could sign after her honeymoon. Vacation. Whatever.

Right now her token gesture to playing it safe was to return to her seat and buckle up. "Well, Madeline and Ashley, what brings you out to Fantasy Island?"

Madeline had the grace to look apologetic as she reached forward and snatched a strawberry from the tray Laney held. "Just me, myself and I. No guy in sight for me, but since I blog about honeymoons, here I am. From what I've heard, the brochures don't begin to do this place justice."

Madeline toasted her with the flute, and then they both turned and stared at Ashley, who stared back and actually *blushed*. Laney got the feeling that was a red-letter day.

"Okay," Ashley groused. "I'm flying solo, too. I won a vacation for *two* and there's no boyfriend, fiancé or husband on my horizon."

Madeline lifted her glass solemnly. "Your secret's safe with me. That's more than I've got. Guys look at me and assume I'm holding out for a white picket fence and a ten-carat diamond. Just once, I'd like to have hot, kinky sex. Not every guy has to be a keeper."

The pilot came on the intercom to announce their imminent arrival. Seconds later the plane banked, and a small island swung into view on the right side. The first thing Laney noticed was the impossible quantity of palm trees—surrounding an impossibly teeny-tiny runway. The ocean flashed outside her window, a light aqua blue dotted with the darker shadows of coral reefs. So far, Fantasy Island was even prettier than its pictures. Laney couldn't wait to see her private villa and check out the two-plus miles of white sand beach.

Madeline leaned forward. "Do you think it's true, what they say about the cocktail menu?" She laughed at the look on Laney's face. "That it's not *really* a drinks selection. It's a list of fantasies. Point and pick. That's all you have to do."

"They can do that?" According to the sleek marketing brochure Laney had read, Fantasy Island advertised itself as a small slice of paradise in the Caribbean Sea— and the perfect place for a honeymoon or a destination wedding. Renowned for barefoot luxury and discreet hedonism, the staff's mantra was *"Pure decadent pleasure."* Any wish. Any desire. If she'd read between the lines correctly, no sensual fantasy or pleasure was off-limits for the well-trained staff that catered to guests' needs. At the time, that had seemed fairly adventurous, but she'd been thinking in terms of beach massages and sex on the sand with her new husband.

Apparently, she needed to broaden her horizons. Live a little. Blah blah blah.

It was some consolation that Ashley looked as shocked as Laney felt. Or not. Because, as the seaplane started a rapid dip and glide toward the island, the other woman grinned, and there was no mistaking the look of glee on her face. "This is going to be awesome."

Laney double-checked her seat belt and wondered, not for the first time, why Harlan had picked this particular locale for their honeymoon. He'd been a grade-A asshole, but maybe the man hadn't been as clueless about their bedroom fun times as she'd believed. Maybe he'd had fantasies and she'd not been enough. Well, screw that. This time the only fantasies that mattered were her own.

2

ON A GOOD DAY, Laney saved at least five lives by noon. Her numbers dipped during the slower weeks, because not all days were a constant rush-rush of heart attacks, gunshot wounds and four-car freeway pileups. San Francisco traffic made the Autobahn look tame, and the off-ramps at Balboa Park alone had ambulances pulling into the bay on a semimonthly basis. Instead of scrubbing in, arms up as she hip-checked her way through the surgery door, however, now she was…naked.

Absolutely butt-naked and stretched out, waiting for a man to come and run his hands over her body.

Usually, naked was cause for celebration, except for the inescapable fact that she was all alone in a cabana with the same grade-A ocean views that had greeted her plane yesterday. Her surroundings included miles of powdery white sand, dotted with palm trees, and nothing but the calm blue Caribbean Sea begging for a close encounter with a snorkel. Fantasy Island—which was a ridiculously *fantastic* name—was undeniably much prettier and calmer than her usual Monday morning gig.

Harlan didn't know what he was missing, the bastard. Oh, he was still a good-looking bastard, tall, broad shouldered and dark haired. He'd been tapped to play football for his college, but by then he'd already decided medical school lay in his future, and he'd passed on the team because he couldn't risk the damage to his hands. If she hadn't taken the Hippocratic Oath herself, she'd have been tempted to step on those talented fingers. Hard.

Imagining Harlan here on Fantasy Island was surprisingly difficult, although he'd been the one to pick out the place for their honeymoon. She was fairly certain she remembered what good sex was like. Or, at the very least, she remembered *having* sex. Decent sex with matching his-and-her orgasms at the end. Since both she and Harlan were trauma surgeons, they didn't share too many off-the-clock hours, and she'd had to schedule time to make love with him, which was a sad commentary right there. This trip had been her chance to *not* be in control of every step of their sex life, and she'd been looking forward to it. While he, on the other hand, had been checking out nurses.

She wriggled on the massage bed and snuck another peek at her phone. Her ponytail slid over her shoulder and she forced herself not to grab it and play with the ends. But holy awkwardness. Lying here like a slab of meat hadn't been in the spa brochure. Her cabana boy— aka *masseuse*—was late. The spa attendant had turned on some kind of New Age crap music, heavy on chimes but missing any noticeable beginning or end. The chiming went on ad nauseum. For added bonus points, the attendant had spritzed the air, and Laney's towel cocoon smelled like some kind of floral scent that made her nose itch.

Waiting was not a good use of time. The sixty hours a

week she spent—*had* spent—in a San Francisco trauma bay had been measured in increments of a minute or less. Of course, the same could be said about her sex life, which was her problem right there. She hadn't been getting any, ergo she had sex on the brain.

Or maybe that was the resort's fault. Her libido had Madeline's explanations on the seaplane playing in a sexy loop through her head. Place an order from the cocktail menu—and pick a sexual fantasy. *A Good-Night Kiss, Affair, Climax, Double Jack, Triplesex…* Pick one. Point. All she had to do was ask for it.

She lifted her head up and fished her phone out from beneath her sheet. Six minutes late. She'd scheduled thirty minutes for this massage business—so she had twenty-four minutes left.

She liked to keep to her schedule.

Her masseuse, apparently, did not share her outlook on life.

"You're cheating, sweetheart. No phones in the spa."

Two big legs appeared in front of her, legs as big and rough as the voice issuing orders. Laney looked up and up and…sweet baby Jesus, the man had good genes. He was also more than a little rough around the edges. His face was all hard lines, his hair cut ruthlessly short with military precision. Dark stubble shadowed his jaw as he towered over her. He wore the loose white pants and form-fitting T-shirt that all the male resort employees sported, but somehow he managed to make the cotton look lethal, as if he were balanced on a razor edge, ready to pummel or go brute predator on the first threat that crossed his path.

This was her masseuse?

He tapped her phone. As if he had the power to make

her do precisely as he commanded. It wasn't hard to imagine him giving orders. Hit man. Maverick CEO. Rogue mercenary. She had no idea who he was, but her body leaped in anticipation when his thighs bumped against the side of the massage table.

Was *he* on the menu?

"This isn't the spa." Since her butt was stretched out beneath a cabana with a thatched roof, building rules absolutely did not apply. Neither did logic since, although Fantasy Island had twelve private villas, all positioned for maximum privacy and sunset views, what it did not have was an actual spa building. She'd been promised her masseuse would be *happy to attend you wherever you wish, madame*. "And you're not in charge."

"You're on my massage table." Amusement colored his deep voice, although his face remained impenetrable. Playing poker with this man would be dangerous. Hell, everything about him screamed dangerous. He certainly didn't fit the spa's brand of peace and mind-numbing serenity. He made the gangbangers, with their frequent-flyer cards to her ER, look like tame bunnies.

"That makes me the client." *And your boss.* After all, she'd be picking up the tab for this little hands-on session.

"Uh-huh." He plucked the phone out of her hand. "What could you possibly need to check?"

"The time. Give me back my phone." She rolled over, sat up, extended an arm, and the sheet promptly dipped to nipple level. Damn it. The spa attendant must have been an Egyptian embalmer in a former life, because somehow the woman had gotten all the individual pieces of sheet strategically arranged to cover the embarrassing bits. Laney could do an emergency intubation on a flatlining patient, but the sheet defied her. She yanked it up and used her armpit as an anchor. *Sexy.* Not.

"You have a hot date?" He pocketed her phone, ignoring her outstretched hand.

Are you busy? "So. Are you going to massage me or what?"

Oops. That sounded downright pornographic. Her girl bits immediately voted for option B even as she lowered her arm.

"Lie down." He nudged her eye covering back down, plunging her into the dark. She didn't do vulnerable—and apparently her credit card wouldn't need to cover a tip for this man because he had zero customer service skills.

"Wait." The blast of heat she felt as she processed his order—and *followed* it—was chemistry. She knew all about chemistry, thanks to medical school. This man simply possessed enough symmetry that her own body had ramped up the pheromone production. It wasn't personal—it was simply that he was mate-worthy.

"Who are you?"

Before he placed his hands all over her naked body—*please*—she needed to know his name.

"Gray," he growled. Since Laney Parker's sweet little butt had intersected with his current mission, exchanging names seemed harmless. Plus, he was fairly certain that a real masseuse would have introduced himself or been labeled with one of those name-tag thingies. His three-day crash course in massage techniques clearly hadn't prepared him as well as he'd thought.

Around her, however, he didn't feel professional. Instead, he'd had a knee-jerk reaction to seeing her spread out and waiting for him. And that was *before* she'd instinctively followed his orders. How far would she let him push her? She wasn't the kind of woman he usually went out with, but there was something about her... *Raw. Vulnerable.* Those were two words that came to mind, although they didn't begin to describe her. She'd looked stiff and uncomfortable, sitting up on the massage table, until he'd ordered her to lie down. She'd liked the orders. Liked being told what to do, being able to shut off the commentary undoubtedly running through her head, and that was just fine with him. He could think of all sorts of orders he'd like to give her. She was unexpected and hot as hell, a delicious bonus he hadn't anticipated finding here on the island.

She also wasn't giving in easily. She'd make him work for her submission. He knew it instinctively.

"Gray, we're going to need to work on your interpersonal skills." She paused and then reached up to remove the cloth he'd slapped over her eyes.

"Leave it." He shouldn't have given her the command, should have let this scenario play out according to her rules, but he'd gotten a good look at her face when he'd confiscated her phone. Her eyes were dark blue, framed by long lashes. She had brown hair and fair skin, with no hint of a tan, so either she was a recent arrival on the island, or she was an overachiever in the sunscreen department. She'd pulled her hair up in a sleek ponytail that made him want to wrap the glossy rope of hair around his hand, hold her in place for his kiss. His touch. The arch of her brows and her stubborn jawline promised she didn't take orders from just anyone, so the question was: Could he make her want it? She shifted uneasily, the ponytail sliding over a bare shoulder, teasing the freckle in the vulnerable hollow. Her eyes were authoritative and cool for someone who was waiting around naked.

"Stay down. I'm not done with you." He pressed his hand against her bare shoulder, encouraging her to roll over. Such a simple touch, his hand against her skin, but she didn't shrug him away or tell him to go to hell.

Instead, she flattened her palms against the white sheet. She had strong, capable hands, the nails neat and short. She'd eschewed polish, but a pale band of skin circled the ring finger of her left hand. She'd worn a ring until recently.

"You haven't *started*. You're late. And I'm not feeling relaxed."

He could hear her mentally ticking off the reasons he'd failed her. It should have pissed him off but instead, her words were a challenge he wanted to rise to. It might be his first day on the job, but failure was never an option.

The orders to infiltrate Fantasy Island and lay the groundwork for a takedown operation had been straightforward. SEAL Team Sigma operated off the books. Gray had two weeks to get his team on the ground and canvass the island before Diego Marcos touched down. Marcos was unethical, ruthless and moving more product through Central America than *coca*. The man shipped weapons with his drugs, and his arms pipeline threatened the political stability of the region. Uncle Sam had more than a few questions to ask Marcos, and SEAL Team Sigma had been assigned the task of bringing the man in.

Alive.

Sometimes the job description sucked. It would have been simpler and safer to take the man down when he landed. A well-placed sniper. A mined road. Hell, a midnight meet and greet in the man's room. Any of those three options worked for Gray. Instead, he got a hostile extraction. Intercept Marcos and move him to US custody. Although selected resort staff was in on the mission, the island's vacationing civvies needed to remain oblivious to what was about to go down—and that meant *not* blowing his cover. He was the masseuse. She was the client. End of story. So what if civilian life, five-star living and gorgeous, classy women were foreign territory?

"Massage time." The words came out more growl than not, so he added *client banter* to his growing list of skills to hone. Damn it. He needed to do some recon *stat*.

She tapped her fingers on the sheet, waiting for something. Damn. Possibly…an apology? Because he didn't apologize any more than he retreated. He was a take it or leave it man. She thought she was in charge right now. Unfortunately, she was partially right.

"You start by introducing yourself," she instructed. "And then you greet me by name and go over the paperwork I filled out so we can discuss any sensitivities or pain points I may have."

It was cute, the way she tried to put him in his place. But he'd been broken and rebuilt by SEAL instructors during BUD/S training, three of the most grueling and physically challenging weeks of his life. The thirty minutes she'd scheduled with him was nothing in comparison.

"Gray. Laney. And you checked no boxes."

A smile tugged at the corners of her delectable mouth, and he wanted to lift the cloth off her eyes himself. See if the smile lit up her eyes like it did the rest of her face.

"Good job." She doled out the praise as if he were

a toddler or a trainee. Boot camp and his military instructors hadn't bothered with the carrot. They'd been all stick.

And then she gave in and rolled over, presenting him with her back. She was all tangled up in her sheet, the wrapping dipping perilously low on her butt. She had a fantastic butt. He could see the soft indentations at the base of her spine. The urge to smile came out of nowhere, as did the sudden need to trace those delicate spots with his fingers.

What the hell was he doing here?

In what universe had Uncle Sam and his superior officers believed a team of SEALs could go undercover as resort staff? From the other side of the pool, safely positioned inside the towel hut, Levi flashed him a thumbs-up. Right. The bastard had slapped him on the back and announced, "Bring her some towels, man, and give her a massage."

She turned her head. "Clock is ticking. Chop chop."

Did she have some place to be? Apparently so, because she held out her hand. "Give me back my phone."

"The phone's in time-out." The words were out of his mouth before he could think them over.

She snorted. "Are you new?"

"You could say that."

She nodded and then opened her mouth and proceeded to give him an unending stream of instructions. "I've indicated a preference for essential oils on my spa form. Medium pressure, but I usually have discomfort in my upper back that could benefit from deep tissue work. Start with the deltoids. Then the trapezius. If you can work my trigger points, I'd appreciate it. I can show you."

She twisted around, her fingers pressing against her back. The sheet slipped. "Lie down."

He resisted the urge to smack her butt. She was as tough as any drill sergeant he'd met at BUD/S but more than twice as pretty. She had that working in her favor. Levi laughed silently from across the pool, and Gray flashed him the bird, grabbing a glass flask of oil from the cart beside the bed. Cardamom and jasmine oil, per Her Royal Highness's orders. He poured it into his hand, warming the slick stream.

"I'll show you." She twisted on the bed again.

"Down," he gritted out. Were ropes allowed in commercial massages? A gag seemed like a useful option, as well. Before she could squirm away from him, he spread the oil over her shoulders. She had the palest skin, dotted with freckles but no swimsuit lines. He reminded himself that skin was just skin. It covered bones and muscles. He'd never thought about it before, but damn, she felt special.

The instant connection he felt when he touched her was unexpected. She sucked in a breath as if she maybe felt it, too. At least he'd shut her up for the moment. Yeah. He was a horny bastard, because he immediately started thinking about other ways to make her hold still. Make her *come*.

He drew his hands down her back in sweeping strokes, working out the visible tension in her neck and shoulders. He was no expert, but her back was a mess of knots. What the hell had she been doing? She was a woman on a tropical island. She was supposed to *relax*. He rubbed his thumbs in small circles, working out a particularly hard knot.

She whimpered, a breathy bedroom sound he'd bet

she didn't know she was making. Better yet, she'd finally stopped issuing directions. He didn't dare imagine whether she'd stripped off completely beneath the towel or if she had on just a pair of panties because he was already hard. He'd gone undercover in the worst biker bars in California, fought hard, ridden fast. A massage should have been easy, but he'd never been so hot for a woman before.

She turned her head and muttered something. He didn't give a damn what it was.

He pressed his finger against her lips. "Not one word."

"Or…?" Sweet challenge filled her voice and, yeah, he wanted to show her. Instead, he worked his way down the straight line of her spine, headed for her ass.

"I have my ways." He sounded like a bad villain. He might as well have rolled over and showed his belly, because she ignored his answer and started talking again, directing him from one muscle group to the other so matter-of-factly that she probably didn't even realize she was doing it. Laney Parker was definitely a woman who was used to being in control. He recognized her need because he felt the same way. But one of them had to give and it sure wasn't going to be him.

"We need to be clear on one thing." He leaned forward, so his mouth was level with her ear. "I'm in charge."

GRAY HAD MAGIC HANDS. Laney should have gone for sixty or even the full ninety minutes instead of the paltry thirty minutes she'd ponied up for. He was that good.

"You're tight here." He pressed a particularly tense spot on her back, and she stopped caring that she was stretched out, bare-ass naked and vulnerable. God, he was good.

"Trigger point." Not, apparently, that she needed to tell him. The man knew what he was doing.

"Are you a doctor?"

"Trauma surgeon." Was that sultry whisper her voice? Because, if so, Gray was definitely a miracle worker. She felt herself melting under his touch and, wow, how long had it been since she'd done that?

He found and pressed against another knot. "So I should call you Dr. Parker."

He moved around to the front of the massage bed. The bed had one of those circle doughnut things that she'd always thought were awkward. She opened her eyes as Gray's feet moved into view. She'd never had a foot fetish before, but he was barefoot, and his feet were sun-bronzed and strong-looking. Those few inches of bare skin made her want to see more. She'd bet the rest of him was every bit as spectacular.

It was probably bad she found his feet sexy. He was just doing a job.

Really, really well.

He gently pulled her ponytail free before running his hands through her hair, pressing his fingertips against her scalp. Maybe she'd been a cat in a former life, because she'd always loved having her hair played with. For long minutes, Gray rubbed small sensual circles against her scalp. She bit back a moan. *Just lie here. Keep still.* She probably wasn't supposed to arch off the table, screaming *more, more, more.* Although she could. She definitely could.

He moved closer, his thighs brushing against the bed. If she lifted her head, the situation could get awkward fast. Thinking about that made her stiffen up again, but then he cupped the back of her neck, pressing and rotating. And oh, sweet baby Jesus, she could feel the tension melting away. The small tugs on her hair sent a prickle of excitement through her entire body.

"Should I call you *Doctor*?" he prompted.

"Laney is just fine." The words rushed out on a sigh.

She stared at his feet again, trying to regain her equilibrium. He'd made her drool, damn it.

"Holding still isn't so bad?" He followed up the wicked amusement in his voice with another sensual tug on her hair.

She didn't know him. She'd never been the kind of woman who had casual sex. Because that was a personal choice she'd made, she reminded herself. Lovemaking was about as intimate as it got, and she'd never fantasized about letting a stranger touch her.

Before now, the traitorous voice in her head said, because evidently she was seriously considering taking her sex life in a whole new direction. Gray's direction. The purpose of coming to Fantasy Island had been to take charge of her life. To be someone different, even if the change was only temporary. She wanted to be fun and flirtatious and, yes, just a little wild. In a few more days, she'd go back to being Laney Parker, MD, but on this island she could be someone else. The kind of woman who made her fantasies a reality.

HE NEEDED TO step back. Laney was a doctor, a paying guest—and a civilian. She was undoubtedly an upright, tax-paying US citizen, and he had no business running his hands over her skin. In fact, he was fairly certain that, Hippocratic Oath or not, she was the kind of woman who'd kill him if he played games with her.

So sue him. He liked that, too.

Because he wasn't playing nice, he tugged the sheet lower, exposing the dimples above the sweet curve of her butt. She hadn't gone completely naked beneath her sheet. She'd kept her panties on, and he immediately wondered what it would take to coax her out of them, because he was a bastard and not nice. And iron-hard at just a glimpse of those white panties and the strip of pale skin above the band. He brushed a knuckle over the topmost edge. She'd be wearing something silky, he decided. Panties that were as simple and elegant as the rest of her.

She lifted her head and he retreated a step. Not because he wanted to—he was a guy, after all, and would be more than happy to have her face pressed against his groin—but because he really wasn't a creeper, and he didn't want to spoil her enjoyment of the massage. Still, he was sorry he'd moved when she looked up at him, hair tumbling around her face, eyes slumberous.

She mumbled something incoherent that ended with *on the menu*?

What. The. Hell. He was a SEAL and a fighter. Bar fight, the government's fight—as long as it involved fists and a beat down, he was all in. This menu business, however, was unfamiliar territory. He had no idea what she was talking about.

"The menu." He gave her words back to her as if repetition would somehow miraculously clear up his confusion. Spa menu? Room service menu? He hated being out of his element.

She blushed, and blood surged to his dick. God. He'd

have given his left nut to know what she'd been thinking. "Never mind. I shouldn't have said anything."

Her phone dinged behind him on the counter where he'd tossed it, and she bolted upright. "Time's up," she announced, looking relieved.

"That's my line," he rasped, but she hopped off the table before he could finish getting the words out. He exhaled and considered his options. He probably shouldn't swing her to a stop, but the way she was hightailing it away from his cabana was far from flattering.

Exercising remarkable self-control, Gray let her go, all the while mentally running through plans in his head. A quick check of the week's schedule revealed Laney Parker had another massage scheduled for tomorrow. In fact, the concierge had been busy, because she had appointments scheduled for every day this week. He grinned. He'd bet she was the kind of woman who kept a date.

Levi strolled over and dropped a load of fresh towels on the bed. "Do you suck that badly?"

It was a distinct possibility. "I'll let you know tomorrow."

"She's coming back for more?" His pal looked understandably skeptical.

He hoped so.

"She mentioned a menu." Maybe Levi knew something he didn't.

"She was hungry?" A frown creased the other man's forehead. No help there. "Or really, really desperate for something alcoholic to drink? Either way, that means you officially stink at being a masseuse."

"Thanks for the vote of confidence," he muttered. "It

meant something. I need to know what before she comes back tomorrow."

Levi shrugged. "Then we'll figure it out."

That was the thing about working as a team. If he needed something, his shooters had his back, the same way he had theirs. Their briefing hadn't mentioned menus. It had, however, emphasized that Fantasy Island was an exclusive resort that catered to couples' sexual fantasies. *On-demand* sexual fantasies between consenting adults. Laney had been blushing up a storm when she'd run from the cabana. What were the odds…?

"You think it's something sexual?" Levi's head had apparently gone in the same direction as Gray's.

"Yeah." It made sense. "It fits."

"Or you're indulging in a bout of wishful thinking." Levi grinned and punched him in the shoulder.

3

Get in.

Take the target down.

Get out.

By the time Gray had crossed the island and made it to SEAL Team Sigma's base camp, he was in control again. He'd ditched the spa uniform for his camo and retrieved his weapons from where he'd cached them. Weapons decorated him like ornaments on a Christmas tree. He had a KA-BAR knife at his waist and a Heckler & Koch MP-5 machine gun holstered to his thigh. The Glock resting against the base of his spine was even more welcome.

In his clothes and his own skin, he was starting to feel like his old self again as he worked his way through the thick jungle undergrowth, concealing his trail. Calm. Detached. No emotions. Check, check and check. Those were normal operating conditions. What he felt around Laney had to be simple attraction, compounded by the fact that he hadn't had sex in months.

Sure, part of him was wondering when he'd see her again and if he could coax her into bed, but the rest of him was back on the job. Fantasy Island—which had to be the most ridiculous name he'd ever heard—was five miles long and two miles wide. Approximately four square miles of that space was jungle. The resort's owners had opted to keep things in their natural state, so it was acres and acres of dense, rugged terrain. The good news was that he doubted any of the resort's guests would penetrate farther than four or five feet inside the mess.

Before he'd made the SEALs team, he'd had no idea so many different types of palm trees could be crammed into one small island. Mother Nature hadn't stinted. She'd parked slender fan palms next to spiny palms that stretched fifty, sixty feet up toward the sky. The island also came with a shitload of coconut palms loaded with ripe nuts waiting to brain anyone dumb enough to make camp at the base. What wasn't palm was Hispaniolan mahogany and muskwood, and there were vines tangled up around positively everything. The place was "lush, pristine jungle" according to the resort's marketing brochure, but a tropical pain in the ass from where he stood.

A lizard darted up a trunk as Gray moved deeper. The place was green, sure, but it was also chock-full of tree snakes, the odd boa and a seemingly endless supply of toads and frogs. It was damned hard to hear himself think. Their team had set up a base camp on the other side of the island. It was their space, a place where they could be themselves and relax. In addition to four camouflaged tents, someone had strung up a couple of hammocks, and there were stacks of supplies, weapons and radios. More than an outdoor rec room, it was also their fallback position, the strip of beach below the camp their designated emergency extraction point.

As he stepped into camp, he was met by the two

shooters he had patrolling the perimeter. Sam and Remy were the newbies on the team, so he'd passed on sending them in undercover. He needed to know how they handled a mission first, before he put them on the front lines.

Sam flashed him a two-fingered salute. Slim and brawny with close-cropped brown hair, he still looked like the Alabama country boy he'd been before he joined the Teams. He was damned good at blowing stuff up, however, and swam faster than any SEAL Gray had ever seen. He also doubled as their unit medic. "Tell me you brought us a cold one."

"Gray's buying as soon as we're Stateside." Levi stepped out of the jungle behind him. Gray's Senior Chief was the first of the infiltrators to arrive, and although his eyes moved from palm to palm as if he expected an army of hostiles to pop out and open fire, the guy sported a big-ass grin on his face. Gray had seen the same grin when they'd been pinned down in Iraq, taking heavy fire. "Waterfront acreage. Very nice choice."

As Levi dropped down onto the hammock Sam had strung up between two palms, looking as relaxed as any weekend warrior in his living room, Mason slipped out of the jungle. Mason was Mr. Silent. The big guy flashed a face full of attitude and was the kind of guy you expected to administer a beat-down in an alley. At thirty-four, he was also the oldest operative on the team and the best damned sniper Gray had ever worked with. He was no cowboy, but he'd made it clear he planned on dying in his boots. You didn't piss him off without having a really good reason. Hell. You didn't piss off anyone on the team. Gray almost felt bad for Diego Marcos.

Remy followed. The Cajun seemed right at home on the island, passing as the general maintenance and go-to guy. He'd be the man in the hot seat when it came to bringing Marcos in because he'd be the first to face the guy.

Ashley was the last to arrive. She'd infiltrated Fantasy Island as a guest and, in keeping with her cover, she entered their bay in a resort kayak, just another guest out for a recreational paddle. Never mind that she'd driven the kayak through the lagoon waters at a brutal pace, taking the craft through the rocks just for shits and giggles. She looked sexy as sin in her skullhead-print bikini and a pair of hot pink shorts that earned plenty of teasing from the guys.

Levi winked at her. "Now that's a get-up you won't catch a SEAL in."

She flipped him off and dropped down onto a stack of duffel bags. "My boobs are better than yours. You'd look damned silly in a bikini."

"Now there's truth, sugar." Levi laughed, unoffended.

Gray let the teasing wash over him as he broke down his gun. He didn't need to look at it—any SEAL could break down and rebuild his weapons in the dark—but he didn't want to watch Levi and Ashley flirting it up, either. He could go back to the resort and find Laney, but he didn't have Levi's smooth charm or way with words.

No. He was empty. Lonely. Itching for the next fight, the next mission. As he watched Levi and Ashley bickering amiably, giving each other a hard time, part of him wanted that. Sure, they drove each other crazy, but they did it together. *Lonely* wasn't on their agenda. All he had to offer Laney was a few nights of sex, however, and that was a different kind of crazy.

He got on the radio for their coded transmission while the rest of the team continued ribbing Ashley. But when

Gray signed off, the team suddenly fell silent, looking at him expectantly.

"We're getting yanked," Levi joked. "Or, better yet, instead of camping out here in the jungle, we've got a week's shore leave and a reservation at the resort. I've seen the food they're serving."

Levi's sweet tooth was notorious. The man always packed Snickers bars in his bugout bag.

"We've got movement on our target. He's under way."

Marcos spent the majority of his time holed up in a jungle compound in the Belizean mountains. The place was a fortress. A well-placed sniper might also have stood a chance of getting off a shot, or the team could have mined the road in and detonated a lifetime supply of C4 underneath Marcos's Humvee, except the man was cautious and rarely moved out in the open. Learning that he intended to come here had been a piece of intel that had taken Ashley's team eighteen months to acquire.

Levi cursed. "Define *movement*."

Gray knew how his comrade felt. "Marcos will be here in eight days instead of ten. His advance team hits the ground in four. We need to take them down fast, as soon as they arrive. And since we're looking to capture Marcos, not kill, we're going to report back as his guys and make sure he feels safe to land."

"A challenge." Mason didn't sound as if he minded. Instead, he had a thoughtful look on his face as he pondered the logistics of a quick, nonlethal takedown on an island that was too small for roads or runways. There were nods of understanding from around the circle. The FBI had a long list of questions for Marcos, and a dead man didn't do any talking. If the mission went according to plan, however, they'd take down Marcos and then have a week to interrogate him before any of his associates realized he'd been compromised.

"Is the advance party inbound by air or water?" Levi asked.

Gray didn't hesitate. "Two helos, both of which are scheduled to be met by the resort's jeeps. We'll put SEALs into the driver's seats. Marcos will be told his advance team is securing the resort. We need to minimize the risk to the island's civilians. Thoughts?"

Ashley picked up the ball and ran with it. Gray was fairly certain there wasn't anything the woman didn't know. "It's low season and the resort is running at about thirty percent of capacity. There are twenty bungalows. Six are occupied, but three of us are singletons. Eight guests are currently in house."

Good. Fantasy Island would be clear before Marcos made his grand appearance. If Monday's arrivals vacated in a week, that meant Laney Parker would be okay and not in the line of fire. She hadn't signed up for this particular battle, and he wouldn't pitchfork her into the middle of it.

As the meeting wrapped, Gray did a last inventory of his team. They were ready, but that had never been in doubt. Despite the teasing and good-natured bickering, every man there would lay down his life for the team. They were organized, well trained and efficient as hell. Marcos wouldn't know what had hit him.

When Ashley stepped past him, however, he snagged her wrist. "I've got a question."

"Anytime." She dropped onto the pile of duffel bags next to him. "Ask away."

"You ever heard of a cocktail menu? A special one?" He took a shot in the dark, because Laney's tone had held a certain something. He needed to know what she'd really meant.

Ashley laughed. "So you've heard about the infamous drinks menu?"

"Give me details." The way she was smiling, he was in trouble. He definitely didn't know enough.

"Well, the next time you boys decide to go undercover at a resort, you might want to pick one that doesn't specialize in kinky sex."

"I'll give my boss a heads-up," he said dryly. "I hadn't planned on having kinky sex on this mission."

Absolutely not. Hell, even plain old vanilla sex was pretty much off-limits. While there weren't hard-and-fast rules about personal activities while undercover, bedding a civilian who could blow his cover was definitely pushing the boundaries of what was acceptable. He couldn't and wouldn't jeopardize the mission.

Or Laney's life.

"Maybe you should rethink your position." She elbowed him, eyes twinkling at the pun. "Because apparently the resort staff can be more than a little adventurous, as can the guests. The names of the drinks are code for various fantasies you might want to act out. It's all secret and hush-hush, a way for guests to discreetly communicate their desires to each other."

Fantasies about sex. That sounded pretty damn erotic, but he'd seen how other people's kinks played out when he'd worked undercover as a biker. M-Breed's members had engaged in frequent sex, often public, and never nice. On the pool table, up against the wall, in a bathroom stall. Take your pick, do whatever the hell you wanted to do. Gray had managed to avoid the gang's groupies, because no way he wanted a woman who was into him only for the drugs or position she thought accompanied sleeping with him. His fantasies were different.

He frowned. "How did she know about the menu?"

Ashley raised a brow. "Which *she* on this island propositioned you? And did you turn her down flat or take her up on it and she shocked your delicate sensibilities?"

"I gave one of the guests a massage," he said gruffly. "She said something to me at the end."

Ashley whistled. "You must give a really good massage. Give me a name."

"Laney Parker." Why was he so reluctant to give up her name?

"She was your client? In that case, I may have told her about it."

"And how come *I* wasn't informed?"

Ashley winked at him. "I didn't think you'd be interested. Not your kind of scene."

He wondered when he'd started coming across as uninterested in sex.

"I don't like surprises," he said. Although he'd definitely liked Laney. If he'd known what she was asking him, he would have followed up. He definitely wouldn't have let her run off on him.

Ashley's eyes flashed. "You're not exactly vanilla."

Neither were most fantasies.

She poked him in the chest. "Do you even know how to flirt?"

Shit. Did he? "I know how to play games," he grumbled.

Levi smacked him on the shoulder. "Ashley's the best. You can take notes."

"This from you." Disapproval radiated from Ashley's voice. "You're the team man whore."

"And you're not on the prowl? I've watched you hanging out by the pool."

"I'm undercover." She jabbed a finger into Levi's chest. "I'm playing a part. Someone has to get in there and keep an ear to the ground."

"Duly noted," Gray growled. "Don't make me put the two of you in time-out. Break it up, move it along."

Ashley blew Levi a kiss and headed back to the beach and her kayak.

"That girl is trouble." Levi shook his head. "Maybe that's why we don't let women join the SEALs."

Gray grinned. "They'd kick our asses, and we like being in charge."

"True." Levi made a face at Ashley's departing figure. "She's damned good at it."

SLIPPING INTO THE water was like coming home. Diving had been one of Gray's favorite parts of BUD/S training. The world seemed different beneath the surface, everything more buoyant and streamlined. The bay was mostly sandy-bottomed and dotted with coral heads. Butterfly fish swarmed him as he dove toward the bottom, bright yellow and black sides flashing. Any closer and the fish needed to buy him dinner first, one particularly bold specimen bumping against first his mask and then his dive gloves.

He'd grabbed the tank ostensibly because someone needed to map the bay's bottom. He could do it, so why not? He was restless. That was all. He preferred to be on the move, to be doing something, and the riskier and faster that something was, the better. Not that checking out the bay scored high in the adrenaline category. The entry was shallow and the water almost currentless. That would change, of course, as he pushed around the promontory and into open ocean, but for now it was easy money.

Swimming out of the bay and around the island's coastline produced no surprises. As he swam, he checked the ocean floor for obstructions, booby traps, anything that would hinder a Zodiac or a landing party. Fantasy Island, however, was as pretty below the surface as it was above, all white sand and the occasional coral head. He was all clear if the second team infiltrated by water.

The last time he'd done this hadn't gone as well. He'd led an amphibious operation to select possible beach landing sites. The aerial pics had shown mangrove, swamp and jungle, none of which made their potential targets vacation destinations. Worse, the nautical charts were one hundred fifty years old and missing major terrain features. Swimming through the surf and the reef to make the inner lagoon had been like diving in a washing machine with blades. Fantasy Island definitely won in the looks department.

When he finally surfaced, treading water two hundred yards off shore with a quarter tank of air left, he shouldn't have been surprised to see Laney. She didn't seem like the kind of person who sat still. He watched, transfixed, as she pounded up the quarter-mile stretch of sand, sprinting barefoot. God knows, he should have submerged and gone about his business, but looking away was surprisingly difficult. Ponytail whipping back and forth, the muscles in her thighs flexed as she worked for more speed, and her swimsuit top…yeah. He liked that part of the view best. She was spectacular. When she reached the end of the beach, she flopped down on the sand. He grinned. Good to know she wasn't Superwoman. Then, when she fished in her beach bag and produced her phone, his grin got even wider. The woman had a serious cell phone addiction.

Giving in to temptation, he swam in slowly, enjoying the sensual way she dug her fingers into the sand, soaking up the heat as she chatted. Then he counted. Wait for it…by the count of thirty, she'd popped up and was pacing back and forth. He should swim away. Reconning the bay was one thing and an acceptable use of his time. Cozying up with Laney, however, wasn't really part of his job description. He wasn't supposed to be here. On the other hand, he *was* a SEAL. Being somewhere unexpected wasn't unusual.

Deflating his BC, he planted his feet on the sandy bottom. Who was he kidding? He was headed straight for shore. Toeing off his fins, he submerged and let the small waves push him toward the beach.

4

"CARSON HOSPITAL DOESN'T have your acceptance letter on file. Tell me you signed the letter."

What were the ethics of lying to one's mother? Three thousand miles apart, and Laney still fought the urge to look over her shoulder, because a stellar international calling plan made it sound as if Ellen Parker were standing right behind her. Tossing her cell phone into her beach bag had been her first mistake. Answering at the *Jaws* ringtone had been her second.

Unfortunately, her mom was a pro and correctly interpreted the ensuing silence. A top-notch hospital administrator and former oncologist, she excelled at detecting bullshit. "That letter is your second chance, Laney Parker. Do you know how many favors I had to call in to get it?"

Laney had a lot of experience fielding unhappy phone calls from her mother. And, in this case, her mom actually had a valid point. Thank you seemed too…bland. Unappreciative. Because, in truth, she *did* appreciate her mother's attempts to fix the disaster she'd made of her medical career.

"I've signed it." She just hadn't *mailed* the letter yet, because that would mean admitting she wasn't going back to S.F. General.

She'd been sacked. Let go. Fired out of hand. No, not fired, exactly, because she'd been politely asked to submit her letter of resignation so everybody could pretend she'd simply decided to exchange her dream job covering San Francisco's busiest trauma bay for the much tamer, less exciting challenges of a small city ER. Her mother exhaled, the sound magnified by a stellar cell phone connection. "Give me the tracking number and I'll follow up on it."

Her mother made no mention of Laney's vacation-cum-honeymoon. Of course, her mother was also a fixer. As was her father. Realizing Laney was faced with a broken engagement, an AWOL fiancé and the general end of life as Laney knew it, her mother had homed in on Laney's unemployed status as the problem *du jour* and, any other time, Laney would have genuinely appreciated the effort. After all, she didn't want to be unemployed and broke for long, especially given what this trip had cost her.

She just didn't want to give up on *all* of her dreams in the span of the same month. And she definitely didn't want to be banished to Stockton and its less-than-riveting medical practice.

You're an adrenaline junkie.

Who had voluntarily stranded herself on a hot, tropical, ultra-boring Caribbean island. She flopped back down onto the sand. Was there a twelve-step program for people like her? Working as a trauma surgeon might be exhausting, and it almost entirely negated the possibility of a personal life—as her ex-fiancé could attest—but she missed her ER rotations. She itched to be doing something other than working on her suntan, and laying the groundwork for a future case of skin cancer didn't cut it.

Today was another postcard-perfect Caribbean day with blue sky and full sun. She crossed her legs lotus-style at the surf's edge, searching for ever-more-elusive inner peace while her mother ran through the next steps in the get-Laney-gainfully-employed-again plan. It was a good plan, but the sand was wet and getting places it had no business being in her bikini bottom. The heat prickling her skin also indicated a pressing need on her part for more sunscreen. Maybe the resort gift shop stocked SPF 700. She'd check it out as soon as she hung up on her mother.

"I'll get you a tracking number," she said.

Her mother's short huff of disbelief echoed down the line as she correctly interpreted *that* promise. "You didn't send it."

"I will." There. She was committed. Stockton awaited and her future was settled. That was carefully orchestrated plan number one.

"You know I just want what's best for you." Her mother took a deep breath. Laney had already heard the speech that followed—multiple times. She didn't need or want to hear it again. No matter how well-intentioned her mother was, she and Laney didn't always see eye to eye.

"Absolutely." Laney counted to thirty, but relaxing was more challenging than she'd anticipated. After all, she was playing singleton on an island designed for couples. Gray's face popped into her head. Maybe he could be convinced to play.

Danger.

Her mother wrapped up her phone check-in to take

her next call. Laney wasn't sure her final *thanks* even registered. Her own phone chirped a reminder that she had a spa appointment in fifteen minutes. She turned off the reminder and tossed the phone back into her bag.

No more massages.

Avoiding Gray? That should be carefully orchestrated plan number two. She had twelve nights left on Fantasy Island, and she'd scheduled approximately two hundred hours of yoga, kayaking and beach sprints. Hot sex wasn't on that schedule.

And Gray wasn't interested anyhow.

"Massages are not good for me," she said aloud. Weren't massages supposed to be relaxing? Instead, she was tense, which might have to do with the unwarranted attraction she'd felt for her masseuse. She flopped down on the sand, feet in the water, hoping a change in perspective would help. The palm tree overhead was sporting a bumper crop of coconuts. Given the way her week had gone, it was all too easy to imagine getting concussed by a falling coconut. She'd seen stranger things in the ER.

A crab scuttled up the side, pinchers waving. Closing her eyes, she replayed yesterday's cabana scene, hoping for a better ending. Nope. Her humiliation was still complete. She'd tried to order a guy off a menu. That wasn't her. And it hadn't been *fun*. She made a mental note to tell Ashley that her recommendation sucked. Or, possibly, she simply sucked at having fun. She certainly needed more practice.

Cracking an eye, she glared at the crab that had paused halfway in its ascent. "I am officially the most boring, least fun person on the planet."

The crab didn't answer. It was probably a male.

It was certainly pretty enough to fit in. Fantasy Island had some of the most gorgeous men on staff that Laney had ever seen. Gray, for example, was supremely handsome if grumpy. He was also reserved, impossibly self-controlled and not much of a talker—but he had magic hands. She could attest to that. And, best of all, he would have been a *temporary* man. When Laney's two weeks were up, she would have been able to board a plane and he would have stayed put, safely left behind on this teeny-tiny island and at least three thousand miles from her new trauma bay. That would have made him perfect because, after her failed engagement, she needed a break from commitment and notions of happily-ever-after.

The gentle tug on her foot was unexpected. She jerked upright, kicking out hard. Had the crab enlisted reinforcement from his crab buddies? Did they stock alligators on the island?

"It's just me," said a gruff male voice. Oh, God. She knew that voice. Its owner had figured prominently in some very racy dreams last night, saying *You're beautiful* while the voice's owner did wicked, wicked things with his fingers. She wasn't sure which had been her favorite part.

"Why are you here?" She kicked out, splashing water at him. She'd liked him better in the dream, probably because she'd been saying sexy, smart stuff rather than staring at him with her mouth hanging open. In response to her complaint, he wrapped a big, warm hand around her ankle and gently tugged her foot to the ground.

"We need to discuss your need for the rough stuff." Seconds later, a body followed the hand as Gray leaned up on his elbows. The man had no personal boundaries at all, because his world-class swim move put him between her legs and gave him a view of her bikini bottom that neither she nor the suit's maker had ever intended. She hoped nothing had shifted. God, this was *so* not how she'd planned her day.

He eyed her prone position on the sand. "Enjoying the beach?"

"Conducting an amphibious assault?" She yanked on her ankle.

His thumb stroked over her ankle. "Not today. This is an assault-free zone."

Right. Not sure how to interpret that remark, she tried to scoot backward but Gray tugged her forward. He might not be much of a smiler, at least not around her, but there was no denying that he was a handsome bastard. She stared suspiciously at him, but his face gave nothing away.

"Do you ever crack a smile?" She blurted the words out and then flopped back on the sand. Wow. Talk about smooth. He let go of her foot, though, so she inched away. Maybe she could keep going until she hit Miami. Or possibly New York. That might be far enough. Because while he didn't smile with his mouth, he did plenty of smiling with his eyes. Like now, for instance.

He stared at her for a moment, a dive mask and snorkel pushed back on top of his head. His dive shorty was partially unzipped and of course her eyes went straight to the vee of exposed chest. It wasn't her fault that he was running around half-naked and wet.

"Move," she ordered. There was only so much awkwardness and worrying about her bikini line she could take.

"You need to learn how to relax, sweetheart." He stood up, waded out of the surf as if the tank strapped to his back was a featherweight, and holy hotness…his wet suit molded itself to every inch of him. And he had plenty of inches. His crotch was now on a level with her face.

"You're staring." Amusement colored his voice. He shrugged off the tank, dropping it onto the sand.

The drinks menu popped right back into her head as she stared at him, a list of erotic fantasies running through her mind on a decadent loop. *Pick one. Pick them all.* It was like opening a box of chocolates and, even though you knew you shouldn't, you were tempted to choose your favorites before someone else came along and ate them. Gray was tough and hard with a side of wild. He wasn't the kind of man you could tame. She'd stitched up his less honorable brethren in the ER chute, tagged and bagged them when they'd been picked off in drive-bys, and had close encounters with large-caliber guns fired too close and too fast. If those males were trouble, Gray was trouble of a different sort. He was disciplined, controlled, lethal. She hadn't seen him coming, in more ways than one. He might be working as a masseuse now, but she'd bet her last dollar it was a recent career change. She understood wanting to reinvent yourself, but his body gave him away, a roadmap of where he'd been. The puckered three-inch scar on his right forearm was a parting gift from a knife. The cut had been deep, but stitched professionally. The thin line on the side of his jaw, however, had been left to heal on its own. He also had a bullet scar in his right calf, with two small puckered entrance and exit points from a close encounter with a large-caliber handgun.

When he dropped down onto the sand beside her, she went on the defensive. "You're not supposed to be here."

She knew she was being rude, but he simply gave her another crooked half smile. "I didn't realize the bay was off-limits to the hired help."

She eyed him again. Yep. He was still mostly naked and all wet. The parts exposed by the shorty were chiseled perfection. He tossed his snorkel and mask up behind him onto the sand and then tugged the zipper of the wet suit down farther. *Yes, please.*

Then he went in for the kill. "Besides, we're seeing each other now on a regular basis, so you'd better not stand me up."

She gaped before recovering. "I'm not late." *Yet.*

He leaned back on his elbows, his arms brushing hers. Was the casual touch intentional? She had no idea, but the move pulled the edges of his wet suit farther apart. That was definitely a bullet scar on his left shoulder.

"How'd you get that?" She reached out instinctively, running her fingers over the scar. The skin was rough and slightly raised beneath her fingertips. Okay. Her feelings at the moment were completely unprofessional. She could admit it.

"It's nothing." He sounded as if he meant it.

"Since when is a bullet wound nothing? The bullet entered here." She circled the mark on the front of his arm. "I'm thinking it was an armor-piercing round. .50 caliber. That's not the kind of gun you usually find on the streets unless you're hanging out in inner Los Angeles."

He shrugged. "I got in the way."

"You weren't always a masseuse," she said and then, when he didn't say anything, "Where did Fantasy Island really find you?"

He turned his head and looked at her. Part of her, the weak part, wished she was more toned, ten pounds thinner, or even wearing something besides her basic black two-piece swimsuit that tied on the sides with *two* sets of strings for extra security. The rest of her figured he could take her or leave her. He was a risk, and she was a woman who played it safe. He didn't seem to mind her less-than-perfect body, though. His expression was heated and more than a little interested, and all her pent-up urges came surging back to life.

"Come on." He got to his feet and reached down a hand to tug her upright. "I owe you a massage and I know you like to stick to your schedule."

"There's nothing wrong with having a schedule," she protested.

He raised an eyebrow, but didn't let go of her hand. "You schedule your day in fifteen-minute increments."

"How do you know that?"

He shrugged. "I may have looked at your phone."

"It's password-protected." Or had been. She gave him a look that'd had recalcitrant patients lying back down.

"You picked an easy password to crack." There was a definite note of accusation in his voice.

"You're saying it's *my* fault you hacked my phone?"

"Not exactly. I'm saying you should pick a stronger password."

"Or keep my phone out of your hands," she muttered. It should have bothered her more than it did, knowing he'd read her schedule. What else had he read? The expression on his face didn't give anything away, and it wasn't as if she had US national secrets or even embarrassing photos stored on her device. "No phones in the spa," he reminded her. He sounded like a hard-ass, but she was pretty sure that was a twinkle she saw in his brown eyes. Plus, it was hard to take him seriously when he was wearing a wet suit. *Half* a wet suit. "Come on."

"Where are we going? Don't you need to take care of your tank?" she asked, falling into step beside him, anyhow. When he let go of her hand, she fought the urge to tangle her fingers back up with his. Helping her to her feet was just him being polite. Maybe it was something all of the island staff did or maybe, God forbid, he'd thought she was stuck on the sand. Or just really out of shape.

"I'll come back for the tank later. You have an appointment for a massage." He didn't seem to be in any hurry to get them back to the resort, picking a path that winded its way through a coconut grove.

"I was planning on canceling." Confession was good for the soul, right?

"Why?"

Because she wasn't stupid. Because she had chemistry with him and had practically propositioned him yesterday, which now topped her list of Most Embarrassing Moments Ever.

He gave her a sidelong look when she didn't answer right away. "Give me one reason. A *good* reason."

"And you'll let me cancel?" Somehow, she didn't think he'd make it that easy. For whatever reason, he enjoyed teasing her. She couldn't quite interpret the expression on his face, either. There was something more than heat in his eyes. He looked possessive. Because maybe he had some fantasies, too, and they involved him *letting* her do certain things. Or *not* letting her... and wasn't that an interesting thought?

They crunched up the path in silence for the next minute. Or, rather, she crunched and he walked silently. The man had serious ninja skills.

"Absolutely not," he said finally, as the resort appeared through the palm trees. "You're on the books for a massage today, and I know you like to stick to schedule."

The walk was shorter than she would have liked, the massage cabanas by the edge of the pool too close. Worse, the pristine white sheets tucked over the padded beds gave her all sorts of tantalizing ideas that Mr. Tall, Dark and Sexy striding along beside her didn't squash. He'd shoved his wet suit down to his waist and the elastic band of some kind of European swimwear was peeking out—Speedo? She hitched in a breath, trying to calm her racing heart. But unfortunately, the water droplets disappearing down his flat stomach didn't make looking away any easier.

Nope. She was definitely in no condition for a massage. "I'm wet."

"You'll dry." He didn't look concerned.

But spa etiquette said she was supposed to shower beforehand. She'd read the rules. Of course, she was also pretty damn sure he was no career spa tech. Plus, he was a lousy hotel employee. He had no personal boundaries, and he hadn't tried to upsell her once on his services.

He pointed to the towel hut by the pool. "Problem solved."

She just bet. Still, a towel wasn't a bad idea. Her bikini was nowhere near enough fabric between her and Gray.

"Stay here," she ordered and brushed past him to approach the counter. To her surprise, he did.

The guy staffing the towel hut wore the loose linen pants and shirt that was the staff uniform. He wasn't as big as Gray, but there was no mistaking the same kind of ripped muscles. Fantasy Island clearly believed in stocking up on the eye candy. The Pool Boy model apparently came standard issue with hazel eyes and dark blond hair growing out of a buzz cut. He watched her approach, a big grin stretching his face. He was the kind of guy you found yourself smiling back at, even if she had just objectified him in her head. Since even wonder boy behind the counter couldn't read minds, she cut herself some slack on that one.

"A towel, please," she said, stepping up to the counter.

He grinned again. "You can have whatever you want, sugar."

Uh-huh. He was trouble, too. He might not have been as hot as her masseuse, but he was still a pretty impressive specimen. Muscled, with that air of awareness that said he'd be in motion, *doing* stuff, if there was threat. Probably while the rest of them were still gaping. He and Gray had that in common. Also, like Gray, he came accessorized with bullet scars, one through the palm of his hand and another on his forearm. "I want a towel. Levi." She read his name off his tag. God, even his name was cute. *Don't smile.* She knew his type. Give him an inch and he'd think he could have her panties off her faster than she could lick her lips.

"Nothing else…for now?" When she shook her head, he reached beneath the counter and grabbed a towel. A third scar from what appeared to be a .22 caliber bullet snaked across the back of his hand in a jagged line. His eyes followed hers, and he shifted his injured hand beneath the towel.

"Where did you serve?" Her inner doctor kicked in. Based on the extensive scarring, she'd guess field dressing.

He gave her yet another flirtatious grin. *Defensive maneuver.* "Right here, waiting for you."

She rolled her eyes. Did he really think that kind of cheesy line would work on her? Still, his scars were none of her business. She took the towel and retreated to where Gray waited for her by the side of the pool.

"Are battle scars a job prerequisite around here?"

He was back to being poker-faced. "Do you have a soldier fantasy?"

Damn it. She hated blushing. So what if she'd daydreamed once or twice about welcoming her man home? It was none of Gray's business. *Deflect.*

"I'm a trauma surgeon, and I've staffed the ER. Patients don't always tell the truth about how they got injured. My patients lied about everything and anything."

"Maybe you asked too many questions. Maybe the towel boy's embarrassed about how he got injured." His hand cupped her elbow, guiding her toward a massage cabana, a heavy weight against her skin. Sure. Confident. Would he position her that effortlessly in bed?

"How do you know how he got injured?"

He gave her a look. "Guys talk."

"You mean you swap fishing stories. War stories. Who has the biggest dick. Etcetera. Oh, and just FYI… whatever he told you, it's likely exaggerated. All guys do it."

He pulled aside the curtain hanging over the door to the cabana. "Inside."

Uh-oh. She probably shouldn't have mentioned the size of his penis. Or thought about soldier fantasies. "Is it safe to be alone with you?"

The muscles in his jaw tightened. "Yes, but I exaggerate."

"Does everyone lie to you?" Gray snapped open the towel while he waited for Laney's answer. Still warm from the laundry, the high-end cotton smelled like some kind of flower. It was a good smell, way nicer than what he usually encountered in the field. There were definite perks to going undercover at a resort. While she'd grabbed towels from Levi, he'd detoured briefly to strip out of his wet suit and into the spa uniform. He had no idea how the real masseuse handled spending his days in white linen. The stuff wrinkled and was hell on the tough-guy image.

She didn't take the hint to lie down, standing in the center of the massage cabana, chewing on her bottom lip. Since he estimated she was ten seconds from bolting, the towel he wrapped around her was excellent insurance. Maybe he could trade the cotton in for some nice ropes. Or silk ties. He'd bet she'd enjoy the slide of silk against her skin, the gentle tug whenever she moved reminding her that she'd given control to him. He'd enjoy it, too.

Laney shrugged. "Being lied to is an occupational hazard of working in the ER. No one likes to admit that they're responsible for their own accident or that they did something stupid or illegal. Take your pick, but bodies don't lie. That guy in the towel hut was shot on multiple occasions."

"You can tell he took a bullet more than once?" He knew that was the truth, but how did she?

"The scars are different colors," she said with a second shrug that threatened her cotton shroud. "The one on his palm is older than the one on his forearm, so not a matching set."

Damn. She was good. It would have been easier if she were less aware of her surroundings.

"So, no matter what he told you, he's been in a fire-fight."

Also true. Levi had acquired those scars during a less-than-friendly meet-and-greet with the Nicaraguan Navy. He had joked that the bullet that had creased his palm was a souvenir. Since Levi had also walked away from that fight, Gray had been satisfied. Sometimes, blood got spilt. As long as everyone got patched up in the end, that was all that mattered..

"Got it," he said. "Everyone lies."

She shrugged again. "Pretty much."

Great. She'd spent her professional life being conned and lied to, and he was doing the same thing. In the name of US national security, true, but the end result was the same. He sighed. There were days his job sucked, and this was definitely one of them.

"Tell me something, Doctor. Why are you here by yourself?" He stepped in closer until his thighs brushed hers. The massage cabana was a cozy space, and he had her up against the massage bed. He liked the way she refused to retreat, the way she held her ground and dared him to keep on advancing. Sex with her would be good. More than good. It would be great, and she would tie him in knots if he let her. Which he wasn't going to do.

She eyed him suspiciously. "Did you look at my reservation the way you did my phone?"

"Would you believe me if I said no?" In point of fact, he hadn't. Ashley had. She was a whiz at cracking databases and sticking her nose where it shouldn't be. He'd asked her to hack Laney's phone, although apparently that had been super easy because Laney had keyed in the password in front of Ashley, and the undercover op's memory for numbers had done the rest.

Laney sighed and tightened her arms over her chest. The move did fantastic things to her bikini top, so it was a pity her beach bag covered the rest of her because he liked looking at her. She wasn't naked and in his arms, but it was the next best thing. Her swimsuit was approximately ninety square inches of wet nylon.

He could have her naked in seconds.

And then in his arms five seconds after that.

Laney stared at him as if she'd just made up her mind about something. She stepped backward and he knew immediately that playtime was over. She was done with him.

"Damn it," she said, and he recognized the regret filling her voice. He had far too much firsthand experience with that emotion himself. "I really wanted this massage, but I'm going to have to pass."

Letting her walk away from him was harder than he'd anticipated. Her flip-flops smacked against the pool deck with a brisk snap-snap, her ponytail flicking back and forth. She didn't so much as throw him a backward glance. *Stay in character.* He didn't need a consult with Levi to know that a real masseuse wouldn't go chasing after a client who had just canceled on him.

Never break cover. Fortunately, he had that iron self-control thing down pat, because the island's newest guest was hands down the sexiest woman he'd ever laid eyes on. Better yet, she was interested in him, too. He had no idea how he'd lucked into that, but he definitely wanted to be the man giving her whatever she wanted.

He'd never been one to take orders in the bedroom—he was best at *giving* them—but some sixth sense told him Laney might be willing to let him be the one in charge. She was stubborn, opinionated and unless he missed his guess, an excellent trauma surgeon. When she wasn't naked on his massage table, she owned her surroundings. He liked her confidence, her self-control, the aura of awareness she projected. It made the possibility of convincing her to let go even more intriguing.

He watched her go, moving double-time. His current position gave him an excellent view of her ass. She walked with a firm, determined stride, but her hips swayed just the tiniest bit as she walked, a sexy rhythm a man had to watch to catch. He needed to let her go. The closer they got, the harder it would be to not blow his cover, especially given her eagle eye for battle scars.

And…who was he kidding? He wasn't interested in playing this smart. He was interested in *her*. He tossed her abandoned towel onto the bed, and hotfooted it after her, knowing Levi would give him shit for weeks.

"I don't want a massage," she said, picking up her pace when he fell into step beside her.

"Okay." He would have enjoyed giving her one, though. Her basic black bikini had double strings holding the sides together over her hips. One hard tug would be all it took to untie the strings and let the scraps of fabric pool around her ankles… "So tell me what you *do* want."

5

WHATEVER GAME GRAY was playing, he needed to find a different playmate. Did he take the hint, though? Of course not. The man was impossibly used to getting his own way. He tucked his hands in those ridiculous white linen pants and sauntered along beside her. He had no business looking so good in those pants.

Then to add insult to injury, he'd asked what she wanted.

She wished she knew.

"We're not having sex," she said, ignoring the frisson of disappointment in her southern regions. Her body was used to not having sex of any kind on a regular basis.

He blinked, but otherwise showed no other reaction. He had gorgeous lashes, thick and dark, the kind of lush her girlfriends wielded a mascara brush to get and more proof that life wasn't fair. Although, since she got to recover from her breakup on a tropical island, she was in no position to complain. Sitting on her couch mainlining Ben and Jerry's wouldn't have been anywhere near as fun.

"I didn't realize sex was an option," he said finally, and she could hear the laughter in his voice.

Great. Not only had she almost propositioned him yesterday and failed then, but she was failing now, as well. Hooking up should have been simple. She said: "Do you want to have sex?" And then he said "My place or yours?" or even just "Yes, please" and they did it and she had the orgasm she needed so desperately. Instead, one of them was screwing this up and it appeared to be her.

"I'm going back to my bungalow." She needed flirting lessons. Or an intervention. Hookup time was over.

"Uh-huh. And where am I in this picture?" His shoulder brushed against hers.

"Not invited," she snapped. Did he need her to draw him a map? She wanted to be alone. Alternatively, he could relocate to Antarctica and put her out of her misery. This was why dating a doctor had made so much sense. They both had crazy schedules and no time. If you wanted to have sex, you penciled it in on the calendar and there was no misunderstanding about what was happening and when.

Except that Harlan *had* misunderstood her, the unwelcome voice in her head said gleefully.

"Because I'd really like for sex to be an option," he said in that deep voice of his. "I'd really, *really* like it."

She jerked in a breath. And, of course, she had to look down so she could see exactly how much he liked it. Which was plenty, judging by the enormous ridge filling out the front of his pants, but he didn't seem embarrassed by his predicament. He should have looked silly in those linen pants with a hard-on, but he was a big, tough, sexy guy…who was turned on by *her*.

"Tell me a fantasy," he said gruffly, his gaze fierce.

She wasn't a storyteller—she was a fish out of water. Expensive resorts weren't really her thing, although she liked pretending she was a sophisticated world traveler who could handle whatever the island threw at her. But that was a *game*. In reality, she had no idea how things worked here. For instance, the poolside misting thing made no sense to her. Why would you want to lie around on a lounger and allow some random stranger to squirt you with Evian water when there was a perfectly good pool not three feet away? And fantasy sex was even more unfathomable.

"Laney." How did he manage to make even her name sound so sexy? He stared at her, focused and intense. She had the sudden feeling that he could describe every piece of clothing she was wearing, the contents of her beach bag and how she'd done her hair. He didn't miss anything. "Help me out here."

She opened her mouth to say something. Surely it would have been witty or memorable. Something scintillating, if the vacation sex gods were smiling down on her. But before she could get the words out, he was helping himself. He backed her into a palm, his strong fingers tilting her face up toward his. So, okay. That worked for her.

"I'm going to kiss you soon." His words were a statement of intent and not a request. Her body sure noticed the difference. She'd always avoided the dominant type, going for guys who were smart and polished. On their occasional free nights, Harlan had taken her to wine bars and dancing, to opera benefits and restaurant launches. Gray wasn't taking her anywhere. Not only was he bossy and domineering, but he *knew* it, too, and he wasn't making any excuses for it. She shouldn't have been so turned on by it, but…she was.

Oh, God. Was she ever. With Gray, she wouldn't have

to give directions or look after her own orgasm. He nipped her lower lip and soothed the sting with his tongue, a bright bite of pain followed by sweet pleasure. He was dangerous.

She sucked in a breath and angled a little bit closer, until her thighs bumped against his. She could *do* this. Be sexy and bold and fun. "How about now?"

"I can do that." His thumb stroked over her lower lip. Good, she decided. But not enough.

She grabbed the front of his T-shirt, inching him closer. "Do it."

Before I lose my courage.

He grinned. "Your wish is my command."

He took over before she could chicken out, pressing her backward as he sealed his body to hers. Thigh to thigh, chest to chest, and all the good parts in between knocking and grinding together. He was so big and so hungry, roughly sweet and demanding as he kissed her. He wrapped his hand tighter in her hair, holding her in place, and damn could he kiss. If sex on a stick had a taste, it was Gray. He devoured her mouth, his lips moving masterfully over hers as he opened her up deeper.

A callused palm skimmed up her side and over her arm. She arched into the touch, goose bumps skittering over her bare skin. How would his hand feel elsewhere?

He reluctantly lifted his head, his brown eyes meeting hers. "Do you want to order a drink? From the menu?"

She didn't think he was talking about cocktails, but she needed to be sure. "You want a drink? *Now?*"

"Off the special menu, sure." His big hand cupped her face, his thumb rubbing slowly over her lips. "But do your ordering soon, sweetheart, because you're killing me here."

"Did someone tell you about the menu?" Yesterday, she'd felt humiliated because he didn't know. Today, his knowing didn't make things any easier because, somehow, that spoiled the fantasy. He worked here. If there really was a menu, of course he knew all about it. Maybe it was some kind of game the island's staff played. Or maybe it was a joke. Because she couldn't imagine this man letting any woman dictate what happened in bed.

"I've been clued in since yesterday. You'd be my first."

"First what?" Because there was no way in hell this man hadn't had sex before even if he hadn't known about the private menu.

"My first fantasy." He gave her a crooked grin that was as sexy as his kiss. The idea of being his *first* was potent. She'd never pursued a man sexually before. Her relationships had all been pleasant, well thought out and with mutually agreed upon limits. One thing was clear, however. If she slept with him, she wouldn't be the one in charge. He'd demand complete submission in the bedroom, and she had no idea why that was so arousing. She'd led operating room teams, run an ER chute with military precision. She didn't *need* to be told what to do. It was simply a craving.

Her secret fantasy.

He lowered his mouth to her ear. "Did you like the idea of picking a fantasy for me to give you?"

Oh. God. She could feel her face burning. "Yes."

"I should warn you. I don't play by the rules. I enjoy my sex raw, and I have it on my terms."

Wow. She blurted out the first thing that came to mind.

"Does that mean you intend to hurt me?"

He smiled slowly. "Only if it feels good."

"To you—or to me?"

"You, sweetheart. It's all about your pleasure in our bed."

"So if I don't enjoy pain, you won't give me pain." Shockingly, she was okay with that.

"I'll give you what you enjoy. You just have to ask for what you want."

LANEY STARED AT him suspiciously, as if he was mere seconds away from tying her to the palm tree and spanking her pretty butt. She rallied fast, though. He'd give her that. "You should know that I'm not into handcuffs and leather. That's not something I've ever fantasized about."

"Fantasies don't have to be elaborate. A good fantasy doesn't have to mean costumes and whips. It's about whatever *really* turns you on."

From the pink flush on her cheeks, he could tell she had something in mind. Maybe talking dirty did it for her. Maybe it was something else. All he knew was that he'd give it to her. He toyed with her bikini strap while he plotted his next move. Her black suit had embroidered flowers on the cups and was tied in a precision bow at the back of her neck. He'd bet one tug wouldn't be enough to undo her. It would take two, maybe three tries before she fell into his hands.

She slanted a glance up at him. "What do you like?"

You. Naked. "I like to lead in bed."

"Oh." She paused, chewed that over. He would have given a million bucks to know what she was thinking about right then. "Are you a…Dom?"

God, she was so cute trying to get that word out. The

blush on her cheeks grew brighter. He leaned in, fitting his body to hers. "If you're asking if I go to clubs and wear leather, only when I'm riding my bike."

"You have a motorcycle?" Her lips parted, her breath catching.

"Do you ride?" He flattened his left palm on the tree beside her head, caging her in place. His right curled around her hip, stroking the soft skin exposed by her suit.

"Motorcycles are dangerous."

"You don't see the fun side of the danger in the ER," he said.

"Road rash. Lower extremity injuries. Ejection into the path of oncoming traffic. Should I keep going?"

"You'd like riding with me. Imagine what it would be like."

"I've *seen* the accidents," she pointed out.

"Shhh." He pressed a finger against her lips. "It's my turn to talk. I put you on the bike in front of me so I can wrap my arms around you. We take off down the road. It's empty, so I can take us fast. The motor vibrates between your thighs as I gun the engine and push us to ninety—"

"You're going to kill us," she interjected.

"You're spoiling my story. When I can't wait to touch you any longer, I pull over onto the edge of the road. We're alone, just you and me, the road and the bike. I lift you off the bike, bend you over the seat and lift your skirt."

She made a face. "I'm wearing a skirt on a motorcycle? Because that seems really stupid."

"This is *my* fantasy, sweetheart. I get your panties

around your ankles and I'm pounding you hard, your hands gripping the bike."

"I think I'd be demanding more foreplay than that." She sounded breathless, though.

He shrugged. "That's one of mine. You tell me one of yours. We can compare notes."

She hesitated. He figured the best way to get what he wanted—*her*—was to keep pushing. She was driven, a perfectionist and damned curious.

"You have to tell me what you want. That's how this game works."

"You want me to beg?" The expression on her face made it clear that begging would happen when hell froze over. Twice. That was okay by him. He didn't want to humiliate or control her, but he fully intended to have the upper hand in bed.

"I want you to tell me what you want."

"And then?"

She liked things spelled out. In fact, she'd probably prefer a numbered list of sex acts. He bit back a grin. God, she was fun. He didn't know if she'd let him sleep with her more than once—he didn't need a memo from the good doctor to understand that theirs was a temporary relationship with an expiration date—so he planned on making tonight count. And count and count.

"And then I give you what you asked for."

"It's that simple?" Yeah, her voice held plenty of doubt. He'd have to teach her that he always followed through and got the job done.

"Try me."

"I'm out, taking a walk, going for a jog. Having a good time at the corner bar. It doesn't matter where, but then I see you. You're watching me and you buy me a drink, which is really cheesy, but you're trying to be nice, so I buy you one back so we're even."

"Does this drink have a name?"

She nodded. "You're a beer guy, but I order you something really girly, with one of those ridiculous names I can't believe I'm saying to the bartender. Fortunately, the bartender's a woman, so she's on my side. She serves you the *Much Fuss for the Conquering Hero* with two parasols and so many cherries on top that you can't even see the drink. And you have to use the little blue straw."

"I'm a good sport." She was that and fun, too.

She grinned at him. "I think so. But then you order me a shot to get even. A whole row of shots. The bartender is laughing, but she's making her rent money off our tips alone and she enjoys a good joke, so she lines the shots up in front of me."

"What did I send you?"

"I have four drinks to choose from. *Bend Me Over*, and I know you're thinking about me, about what we could be doing. It's not a bad offer, but it's not my fantasy tonight."

"Classy of me. And the second shot?"

"*A Tender Touch*. Tequila, peppermint and Tabasco. It's not what I want. I don't want sweet."

He could feel his lips tugging upward. "At least I had enough taste not to send you anything named after body parts."

"The third shot is *Leather and Lace*. Jack Daniel's and peach schnapps. I like the bite of the first and I've always loved peaches."

He leaned in, his mouth almost brushing hers. "And do you choose any of those three?"

She nipped his lower lip. "I drink the fourth shot, Gray. *See You in the Morning.*"

Well. Hell. While he was still processing that, she up and left him.

MADELINE AND ASHLEY were waiting for Laney when she finally staggered out of her bungalow the next day. Okay. They were lying in wait and so what if she'd slept until almost noon? She'd been up tossing and turning all night, thanks to Gray's fantasy bombshell, and it was her vacation, after all. She couldn't remember the last time she'd slept past 6:00 a.m.

Maddie waved her over to the bar. The bar had a roof made out of palm fronds and swings instead of seats, so you could dig your toes into the sand and knock back margaritas at the same time, which was pure genius.

"Did you do it?" Maddie rocked forward on her swing, almost falling off. "I demand details."

Ashley handed her a margarita. "That's not an *I just got laid* expression. That's the *I tossed and turned all night because he was a dick* look."

"Bummer." Maddie exhaled and nudged the basket of chips over.

"He wasn't a dick," she blurted out, before her brain reasserted control over her mouth.

"Good to know. I'd hate to have to kill somebody." Ashley's mouth curved up in a smile. "So why do you look as if your puppy died?"

"I don't think I'm cut out for this," Laney sat down cautiously on the empty swing next to Ashley. It wobbled slightly, but didn't dump her in the sand.

"What makes you say that?" Ashley slurped up the

last of her margarita and signaled for a new one. The girl sure could knock them back.

"Because she didn't have sex last night." Maddie dug into the chip basket. "That makes at least two of us."

Ashley shrugged. "Me three, but I could get some if I wanted."

Maddie threw a chip at her. "Let's practice our humility, shall we?"

"It's sex…not rocket science. If you're interested, you tell the guy. Or, better yet, you show him. Most of them need the dots connected for them and that's where the drinks menu comes in. You point him toward your fantasy *du jour* and skip the awkward stage where he's trying to figure out what you like, and you're trying to figure out how to politely tell him it takes more for you than a little breast groping and rub-a-dub-dub."

"*Rub-a-dub-dub?* Really?" Maddie shook her head. "I don't think you're going to be scoring in the man department if that's how you see things."

"Their loss." Ashley accepted her new drink from the bartender then swung back toward Laney. "Do you want to hook up with Gray?"

"Yes," she answered. *Yes, yes, yes.*

Ashley studied her over the rim of the glass. "Men aren't that complicated. Point. Pick. If you think he needs directions or you'd find it fun, ask him to re-create a particular drink with you. Just pretend you're at improv class and it's your turn with the bag of props."

Her new friend was oversimplifying things. Wasn't she?

"Think of a drink name," Ashley went on. "Then think of Gray. If the two go together like peanut butter and chocolate, you've got your green light to proceed."

Pick a drink. She could do that. Sex on a beach? The fantasy appealed, but the practicalities of outdoor sex seemed overwhelming. Plus, sand in her girl bits? No, thank you. Up against a wall? Her inner thigh muscles screamed in advance, and she'd have sore spots the size of China from banging against the drywall.

So what *did* she want?

It wouldn't exactly be mind-blowing to invite him back to her bungalow for a night of missionary-style sex underneath the covers. Not that comfort sex wasn't appealing, especially with Gray, but this was her chance to try something new. To be bold and daring and take the new and exciting Laney out for a quick test-drive. After all, if the night turned awkward or embarrassing, she could simply hide in her bungalow until it was time to board the seaplane and leave. She never had to see him again.

Groaning, Laney took a big gulp of her margarita. When had this thing with Gray suddenly become so damn complicated? He'd asked her what she wanted— and what she really wanted was to *not* be the person who had to come up with the night's creative sexual agenda. What she wanted was to be *taken*. To not have to plan, orchestrate or otherwise tell him where to touch and how and for how long. Because she was so sick and tired of that.

She slid Ashley an envious look. Switching places with Goth Princess for a night would be perfect. Anyone, really, other than herself. Someone sexy and confident, the kind of woman who took the man she craved and didn't worry about her love handles or how she performed in bed. It was sex. Not a job, she reminded herself. No performance review at the end.

"I want to be some man's fantasy woman." Just once. Or possibly more than once, depending on how good the sex turned out to be.

"Amen." Maddie licked salt off the edge of her margarita glass.

"Correction. You want to find yourself a fantasy man because what you want comes first."

Ashley had a point. "I deserve a fantasy man," she clarified. Because damn it, she did.

"Agreed. Now tell us why." Ashley gave her the devil's own grin. "Because I smell a story here."

"It's the usual story. Newly minted doctor meets handsome older doctor and falls for him. He invites her to move in to his swank city condo, pops the question, provides a Tiffany's ring and sets the wedding train in full motion." Her breath hitched in her throat but she forced herself to go on. "Then one day our heroine makes an unscheduled lunch stop at her doctor's office and discovers he's already made alternate lunch plans with a nurse. Plans that involve going at it on a gurney with his pants around his ankles."

The mental image was burned into her head. Harlan, pants unzipped, slamming into the nurse. The nurse's ankles digging into his butt as she held on and chanted his name. It had looked uncomfortable—and neither one of them had cared. They'd been too busy having the orgasm of the century. He'd never lost control with Laney like that, never so much as suggested they sneak off and have workplace sex.

"No one looks good in midthrust," Maddie observed, taking another swig of her margarita.

"After I discovered them, I may not have closed the door," she admitted.

Ashley's grin got wider. "Revenge. I knew we were friends for a reason."

"And I may have paged the entire trauma staff to the room for a code blue." She might as well admit the whole embarrassing truth. Rather than suck it up and retreat with her dignity intact, she'd made sure the entire hospital staff knew what had happened.

"Caught in the act. Nice. Me, I'd have gone for something slightly more violent." Ashley shrugged. "He's lucky you're so nice."

And that was the truth, too, wasn't it? She was *nice*. The furthest thing from fantasy material you could get. She worked hard, always kept her word and didn't cause trouble. She'd let the hospital board convince her to resign "because things would be awkward" when she should have fought for what she wanted. And she did have a hard time asking for that. Maybe it explained the lack of excitement in her sex life, too.

"He had his fantasy nurse," Maddie said. "The question is—who are you going to have?"

Gray came to mind.

"Rebound men are dangerous. I'm not having sex just to get even with Harlan."

"Of course not. " Ashley helped herself to another handful of chips. "You're going to have sex for *you*."

Meaning what, exactly? That it wouldn't hurt to treat herself to a rebound man if she went into it with her eyes open?

"Gray likes you," Ashley said with a wink. "Use him."

She suddenly knew how Eve felt when confronted with the apple. Okay, she'd do it. "I'll ask him out on a date."

Shoot. She hadn't sounded particularly confident, had she?

"Is that what we're calling it these days?" Ashley winked. "Go get 'em, tiger."

6

ASHLEY PULLED GRAY aside as he slipped back into the resort. He suspected she'd been lying in wait for him, which was an interesting development. He'd just finished check-in and patrol, and the mission was on schedule. Whatever she had to tell him, it wasn't related to the job.

She nudged him into a laundry room. "Hot date?"

Christ. He hoped so. It was none of Ashley's damn business, however, but when he opened his mouth to tell her so she cut him off.

"Good," she said.

He blinked at her. Say what?

"Laney is in desperate need of a night of really hot, no-strings-attached sex."

He leaned back against the washer, arms crossed. "Understood, but I'd like to know why *you're* telling me this."

"Sorry, Gray. Girl code says I keep what I know to myself."

"I could pull rank on you." They both knew he wouldn't, however. It wasn't how he rolled. If Ashley believed what she knew could affect the mission, this conversation would already be over and he'd have the information he wanted. Which meant this was personal.

She jabbed him in the chest again. Harder. "I work for a different branch of the government."

"You're part of my team."

She sighed, poked him one last time and then gave up the information. "Laney's just come out of a bad relationship. She wants to flap her wings a little, and I applaud that."

"I hear a *but*."

"So I want her to have fun, not get hurt."

He stared at her. "What do you think I'm going to do?"

Because they were on the same page. The last thing he wanted to do was hurt Laney. He wanted her to have fun, too.

"Just be careful with her feelings, okay? She wants to have hot vacation sex and then get on the plane home. You're her temporary man."

"Her temporary man," he repeated. Okay, that was a new way of looking at things. The hot sex part he was on board with, and *temporary* worked for him, as well. He didn't do relationships. Laney didn't want one. No problem.

"The last thing she needs is another guy getting serious about her," Ashley added pointedly.

"Do you see me on one knee?"

Not that he was necessarily averse to the institution of marriage, but he'd never thought of himself and holy matrimony in the same sentence before. He didn't have it in him to make that kind of emotional commitment to a woman.

Ashley elbowed him. "You'd be lucky if Laney let you propose, but no, I know she's safe from you. Her last guy was a jerk. She caught him cheating on her with a nurse three weeks before their wedding. So she doesn't need another guy getting serious when she's still getting over the first. All she needs is hot breakup sex."

"Thank you, Dr. Ruth. You're not concerned about what I need?"

She shrugged. "You're a big boy, and Laney's fantastic. I'm sure you'll get exactly what you deserve."

Uh-huh. "Is that why her reservation was for two?"

Ashley made a face. "Yeah. He made her book the honeymoon, and then he couldn't be bothered to show up. I'm glad she came, anyway."

He was, too.

DATING WAS GOOD.

As were casual encounters, opportunities to get to know each other and anything other than immediately ripping off his clothes and having her way with Gray's body. Sure, the naked Gray fantasy made Laney quiver, but the reality was that she needed to get to know him better before *she* got naked. She hated the awkwardness of the cocktail menu hookup, of not knowing whether he'd found the setup as humorous and exciting as she had. She'd also woken up worrying that every staff member she passed knew she'd tried to order sex off the menu. God. That sounded sleazy. Or desperate. And yet it hadn't really been any of those things, had it?

When she'd told him the story about the shots, she'd been able to take on a different persona. Someone who knew what she wanted and wasn't afraid to tease or play. She liked that person. And yet, when she'd run into him that morning—okay, after she'd stalked him and caught him by the massage cabanas, but he didn't have to know that—she'd been tongue-tied. So much for her suave, sexy side.

Her brain went AWOL around Gray. She'd stood too close to him, gazing into his gorgeous brown eyes and inhaling the scent that was uniquely him. That part had been good, but she'd also been at a loss for words. He hadn't seemed in any rush, though. Instead, he'd waited for her to get to her point.

"Look, I'd like to see you later, when you're not working." Yep. That was what she'd finally said. *Wanna go out with me?*

He hadn't blinked, just rolled with it. "Okay. Give me the when and the where. I'm free any time in the afternoon."

And so here she was, off for a little hike up to a scenic lookout point. Given that the path only went about a half a mile up, it was more of a stroll than anything, but the resort brochure claimed the views were spectacular, and it wasn't as if she could take Gray to the movies. This was also her best chance to get to know him better since massages didn't exactly lend themselves to intimate conversation.

The lack of details hadn't bothered her before, but now she'd had a night to think on it and, it turned out, sex with a stranger wasn't in the top five of her fantasy list. In fact, it wasn't on there at all. She was a chicken. A horny, guy-less, had-a-date-with-her-vibrator chicken.

Ten minutes later, she was standing at the bottom of the trail. Tilting her head, she looked up. The path was definitely more hill than mountain, but the abundance of palms sprouting from either side of the dirt trail guaranteed they wouldn't roast. Gray materialized out of the jungle, and her temperature soared. Maybe he knew a secret employee shortcut because one minute she was alone and the next he was standing there in front of her. He'd dressed for the part today, too, in boots, cargo pants and a form-fitting black T-shirt.

"Very American commando," she said, mentally adding a fantasy about military men to her to-do list.

"I'm a man of hidden talents." He braced a broad shoulder against a handy tree and assessed her clothing. She took the opportunity to stare at him one more time. He was definitely worth a second glance. Her shorts and sneakers must have passed muster because he nodded his head, turned and headed up the path.

But she got to follow his spectacular butt, which was no hardship. He made an effort to talk to her on their way up, too, which she appreciated. He struck her as the kind of man who powered through a hike, with the goal of making it from the bottom to the top in record time. Or at least first. She'd bet he was usually the best when it came to physical competitions, while she admittedly wasn't the most physically-fit woman on the planet.

He didn't seem to mind her slow chug up the hill behind him, however. He adjusted his steps to fit hers and pointed out various pieces of flora and fauna. By the time they neared the top, she'd admired a bright yellow allamanda, a flowery stalk of something flaming red and a particularly large bougainvillea snaking its way up the spiny trunk of a palm tree. A wild monkey peeked out of a palm, chattering madly. The mini-hike was…nice. Not sexy. Not daring or erotic. But nice. It was also a teensy, welcome step forward in her *get to know Gray better before jumping his bones* plan.

As if he'd read her mind, he looked over at her, slow-ing his pace so she was walking beside him on the path. "You hanging in there?"

"I am," she said, surprised to find it was true. She wasn't nervous anymore. Chalk one up for her.

She was ready to do this. She really was. She was going to embark on a fun, exciting adventure with this incredibly sexy man and maybe, when it was over and she was headed back home to her new life of boring, she'd be a different person. The person she wanted to be.

The view from the top of the hill was stunning, the impossibly blue water of the Caribbean spreading away from their island. A few small waves broke on the beach below. She could almost see the strip of sand where he'd surprised her the other day, and the darker shadows of the coral heads promised good snorkeling. *Later.* Right now, she had herself a man to tease. The resort had positioned a romantic daybed for two near the edge of the lookout. The whole place reeked of romance, and her heart gave a little pang.

"So," she said. "We're here."

She dropped down onto the cushions of the seat, her butt sinking into a pillowy softness that practically demanded she drag Gray down for a kiss. Or more. After all, the daybed was definitely big enough for two. They were outdoors, but she could be talked into indulging in a little fantasy action here. Surely they could hear anyone headed up the path in time to cover up. It could totally work.

Instead of joining her in the center, however, her big, brawny masseuse hesitated. Yep. Whatever he had to say was going to be good. Or, more likely, really, really bad.

"Just say it," she advised. "Don't lead up to it."

He rocked back on his heels. "Wow."

She shrugged. "There's no time to sugarcoat in my job."

"That's good." He gave her another one of those crooked half smiles that made her melt inside. "I'm not good with pretty words."

Funny. He'd done just fine so far. But whatever. She wanted to have her wicked way with him, possibly beginning with sex on the daybed, so she wasn't going to quibble with his word choice.

"I'm not looking for happily-ever-after," he continued gruffly. "I need to make that perfectly clear."

Uh-oh. Had he misunderstood her? Did he think she was shopping for a replacement ring? "Did I ask for that?"

He shook his head. "No, but—"

She cut him off. "I don't believe in love." Not anymore. "It's a chemical thing."

"Uh-huh. You're a doctor."

She narrowed her eyes at him. "What does that have to do with anything?"

"Don't they cover the scientific theories of love in those medical textbooks of yours?" He looked genuinely curious.

She went on the offensive. "Do *you* believe in love?"

"I don't *not* believe in it, but it's not something that's ever made an appearance in my life."

He didn't sound as if he'd missed it, either. He had to be one of the stillest people she'd ever met. He dropped down next to her in a lazy sprawl, not moving a muscle, and yet she knew he hadn't missed a thing. A parrot landed in the tree overhead, and his eyes tracked the movement briefly before returning to her face.

Remember the plan. "Tell me more about yourself."

He shrugged. "I have no idea what you want me to say."

That was the thing about guys. They seemed to think that she had expectations that the truth—or just whatever random thought was floating through their heads—would shatter her. When all she really wanted was to hear what he was thinking. It didn't have to be profound or dressed up for her benefit.

She hitched closer to him. "For example, tell me about your last date."

"You want me to discuss another woman?"

Well. Apparently, his face *could* show emotion, because he looked vaguely horrified. Had the date gone that badly? Looking at him, she assumed his last evening out had ended in bed. She didn't want a blow-by-blow account, but she did want to prove her point. She'd bet he hadn't been looking for love then, just a good time. So why couldn't he do the same thing here, with her?

"Details." She leaned back on the mound of pillows and toed off her shoes. She was seriously out of shape if her feet hurt after a half-mile hike.

He folded his arms over his chest. "Only if you tell me about your last date."

"Is this a game of *you show me yours and I'll show you mine*?"

He gave her a slow smile. "Or, we could just play doctor."

She made a face. "You have no idea how many times I've heard that one."

"It doesn't work?" He grinned at her, a real genuine smile splitting his handsome face, bringing it to life.

"I'm here and I'm single," she pointed out. "You do the math, but you still get to tell your date story first."

"I don't date."

Right. Pulling teeth here. "You're telling me you've never gone out and had sex? That you're a virgin?"

Because she *so* wasn't buying that one. She might be sex-starved, but she wasn't stupid.

He laughed. "The last time I hooked up was with a gal I met at a biker bar. There was nothing romantic about it. I bought her a beer. We danced a time or two. Then I gave her a ride on my bike, and we…"

He gestured with his hand and, oh boy, she got the idea. He'd taken his newfound friend outside and done her. On the bike, over the bike, near the bike—she should really find out.

"You like your bike."

"You bet." He watched her so intently, his eyes hooded. Did he expect her to run screaming? Things had been simpler when they were kissing. He couldn't talk. She couldn't think. It had been *perfect* and she needed to re-create that moment. Stat. Unfortunately, he was still talking. "Is this another fantasy of yours, hearing me talk about having sex with someone else?"

Dirty. Out of character for her. Either or both labels applied. It definitely was *not* the sort of conversation she'd ever had with Harlan or anyone else at the hospital, so she went for honesty. "Think of it as a preview of coming attractions."

He smiled roguishly. "I can work with that."

"But you need to know something, too. This isn't me."

THE DAYBED CURRENTLY hosting Gray's ass looked like something straight out of a bridal magazine. It was romantic as hell and positioned for kisses at sunset or for wedding photography. Not that he had any idea how a bride would traipse up here in one of those big, puffy dresses his former teammates' fiancées typically chose. The poor woman would get hung up on the palms and the vines.

The truth was, he sucked at dating. Threading his fingers through Laney's, he tugged gently. She landed hard on his chest with an audible *oomph* and he grinned. She didn't hold back.

"You feel plenty real to me," he said. "Or was that you outing an alternate personality when you said *this isn't me*? Because that could definitely be a deal killer."

"This is a fantasy. A game. One night…no strings. In real life, I'm not that woman, no matter how much I'm going to enjoy being her for tonight." She offered him a solemn smile.

"And what if I want more than one night?"

His voice sounded gruff, and he had no idea where those words had come from, because he'd just finished telling her that he wasn't playing for keeps. He eyed her cautiously, wondering what it was about her that made him want to be different. Why wasn't he halfway down the hill by now?

"I made a reservation. I've only got so many nights."

"Then I want all of them." *Stupid.* Because he couldn't, shouldn't make promises. It was easy to imagine her in a white coat, making rounds with cool competence, but raunchy sex with a virtual stranger? Yeah. That seemed like a harder sell, because she'd have to unbutton and strip down. Let him in. He brushed his thumb over her collarbone, because it was a pity to be this close to her and not touch her.

"And then I go home." She stared at him expectantly.

"Sure." Getting started on those nights suddenly

seemed like a great idea. He brushed his thumb over her cheek, leaning in closer because he needed to know her answer.

"What fantasy would you pick tonight?"

LANEY WAS WET. She wanted more kisses. And she *definitely* didn't want to feel alone in needing more from him.

So why was she still fully dressed?

"I need an answer." His mouth hovered inches from hers, though, as if negotiating wasn't what he had in mind. Good. She had big plans for that incredible mouth of his, plans that involved sliding her tongue along his lips and then possibly nipping at his lower lip. Biting him. She wasn't sure of the details of said plan, but how hard could it be to figure out? She gave it five minutes tops before he lost his clothes.

But then he didn't kiss her again, which was a damn shame. Somehow, she had to spell her fantasy out for him. She inhaled, but the air didn't help. Instead, she smelled Gray, a scent that was all male underlain with the tang of something metallic and the sea. Whatever he got up to in his spare time, it didn't involve patchouli oils. She could imagine him outside, running or pounding through the surf. He was the kind of man who pushed his body hard, not accepting any weakness. If he'd been a caveman, he'd have been the best catch, the leader of the pack and the baddest-ass hunter of them all. He was going to be *hers*, and how awesome was that?

"You have to ask for what you want." *Sex on the beach.* Gray's money was on that particular drink. They were at a tropical resort, and he had a beach handy. She certainly wasn't going to be picking anything with a classy name like *Screw Me Sidewise*. Not that he'd actually be able to figure out the logistics of that one.

"Leather and Lace." She peeped up at him.

"Say that again?" She'd better be *lace* in this scenario.

"Leather and Lace," she repeated, and this time there was no mistaking the pink in her cheeks. Her chin went up and she glared at him. "You asked me what I wanted. That's it."

"Give it to me in detail." He could use a few more words here, plus she was digging into his chest as if she meant to nest. And, like the discussion of semi-permanence, he didn't mind that, either. "You want to play dominatrix?"

She shook her head. "I don't want to tie you up."

Thank Jesus, because he didn't know if he could go that far for her. "You want *me* to tie *you* up?"

That he could definitely do—and he would enjoy every single minute.

She chewed on her lower lip. "Not exactly."

Yeah. He really needed an instruction manual here. Or at least a list of her don'ts.

"I want you to take charge," she said in a rush. "I want you to take *me*. Pin me up against the wall or on the bed and strip me bare and ride me hard."

Wow. "You liked my biker fantasy. You fantasize about rough sex."

"No. Maybe. Not hard enough to hurt, but enough that I feel you between my legs tomorrow, and maybe the day after. Enough that I'm not thinking of anything but you and I'm not in charge, but just along for the ride. I want to let go and not worry about orchestrating some big sexy scene. You'll make it good for us both." The certainty in her voice was the sexiest thing he'd ever heard. "All I'll have to do is enjoy it."

As fantasies went, it was pretty tame. He could think of a few variations, except…it was hot as hell she'd said anything at all to him. Laney had picked out her sexual fantasy, and now she wanted to reenact it—with *him*. Not some anonymous guy, but him. He didn't play at sex and he didn't talk pretty—sex with him was gritty and real, and the women he slept with wanted the same thing he did. He had nothing to offer but straight-up, rough pleasure because he was empty. Tapped out. An emotional well run dry. He was no bloody poet, either, or he could have found some polite way to warn her.

The bottom line was, he couldn't keep his hands off her. Hell, yeah, he was ready to enlist to help her score that fantasy she craved so badly. Not so much because he needed to maintain his cover—although he was pretty sure that factored into the decision somewhere—but more because something about her undid him.

So to hell with it. He rolled over, pinned her beneath him and kissed her. To make his point, he gripped her ponytail with his hand, tugging just hard enough that she knew what he was doing. Her eyes widened, and her breathing grew ragged, which was all the *yes, please, more* he needed.

He kissed her, a quick, hard kiss, and she opened up sweet as sin beneath him, her tongue tangling with his. A down payment on the fantasy he'd promised her. A sneak peek of the night's coming attractions. He was supposed to be the one calling the shots, but she let him in, her mouth sweetly submissive, and who *knew*? He wasn't in control of their kiss anymore. And he *liked* it.

Gray pulled back, sliding his mouth away, his gaze locked on Laney's. Holy. Wow. The man packed a whole lot of sexy into a rapid-fire kiss. She managed to keep herself from demanding an instant replay, but barely. Proposition? Check. Hot kiss? Check. Sexy removal to the bungalow for wild, crazy sex? That part she was still working on. Ask him to carry her, and the man, no matter how buff, was likely to have a heart attack. Piggyback? Fireman style? Just thinking about navigating the path back to the resort gave her a serious case of the giggles.

Gray tugged her to her feet and pointed them both downhill. "What's so funny?"

"Having sex is so much simpler with a bike. You leave the bar, you get on the bike, mission accomplished."

"You don't ever stop thinking, do you? Next time I'll bring my bike." But that slow grin was back on his face. "I prefer a challenge. How about this?"

He wrapped an arm around her shoulders, tucking her into his side. It was natural to slide her arm around his waist. They descended a hundred yards.

A hundred yards later, a new thought popped into her head. "What if someone sees us? Will you get in trouble?"

He gave her a look. Right. Hello. *Secret sexy drinks menu.*

"Do you mind?"

She had no idea. It would be awkward—not to mention downright embarrassing—if the other people on the island thought she'd been reduced to ordering a guy off a menu. Like she couldn't get her own date.

"It's a game, sweetheart," he said softly. "A fantasy. Don't overthink it. If it works for us and you enjoy it, the rest of the island can go screw themselves."

Poetic and insightful up until the end.

"This path is relatively isolated, and the bungalows

are sited for maximum privacy. There's no line of sight from one to the other." A frown creased his forehead. "Which is an oversight. Anyone could get into your bungalow, and resort security would never know."

When they reached her bungalow, she fished in her beach bag for the keys. Overcautious, perhaps, to lock her door on a teeny-tiny private island in the Caribbean, but old habits died hard.

"Can I come in?"

He was giving her one last chance to back out, to change her mind. She looked at him and she knew. She was going to do this. For herself. Just once, she was going to be wicked and daring and do what she wanted. Tomorrow could take care of itself.

"Yes." One word. Funny how potent a single syllable could be.

The key slid through the lock strip and the light flashed green. Good to go. She stepped inside and he followed, the door closing behind them with a soft click. He turned the lock as she toed off her sneakers, thinking fast. Did she strip everything off? Invite him into the shower? Darn it, she should have thought this through more, maybe asked Ashley what *she* did when she brought a stranger home and then copied her.

"Laney," he rasped, and she knew then the doubts didn't matter, because he'd started on her fantasy and she wasn't the one in charge anymore. He was going to give her exactly what she'd asked for.

"Hands on the wall," he ordered, and how could four words be so seductive? He laid his fingers over hers and just stroked for a minute, giving her a chance to sink into the rough-soft feel of his hands moving over hers. It was an unfamiliar sensation, having his big body pressed up against hers so tight she couldn't step away. She should have felt suffocated. Dominated. And she did feel that last sensation, but God, it was hot. He was letting her know that he was there.

"If you want to stop, you tell me to stop." He brushed her cheek with his fingertips. "I need us to be clear on that. Can you do that for me?"

His body enveloped hers, close enough she could feel his cargo pants brush the backs of her bare legs. Finally, *finally*, she didn't have to do anything. All she had to do was let go and feel. And he made her feel so much, starting with the ticklish sensation of his army pants. Maybe they could play soldier next. God, that could be good, too. She sensed he'd let her explore her fantasies for as long as she wanted to. Stretching up, pressing her fingertips against the wall to steady herself, she pushed back against him where he was hard for her.

"You're going to do what I say." His mouth was at her ear, giving her the rough words she wanted so badly. "Not because you don't have a choice, but because you want to. All you have to do is let go and let me take care of you."

"Promise," she whispered. White plaster danced before her eyes, the fan stirring the air in lazy strokes overhead. She was adrift, waiting. Waiting for him to touch her. To please her. It felt strange to be passive, but it was strange-good. There were no worries about whether or not he came or how long it took her. This was *her* night. Her fantasy.

Lips brushed her ear, withdrew. "Don't move your hands."

She wanted to ask *or what*, but he'd tell her and sometimes imagining was even better. He could tie her in place with the terry cord from her bathrobe. Pin her wrists in one big hand. Or land a small, hard slap on her butt, leaving a rosy-red souvenir of his possession. Those weren't fantasies she wanted to bring to life, not tonight. They were a delicious secret.

"You're thinking again," he said.

"True." It was hard to keep her fingers still and flat on the wall when she could turn around and touch him. Explore his hard, muscled chest. Drive him crazy, too, so that she wasn't the only one out of control. Instead, she stood perfectly still. Waiting.

For him.

"You're going to tell me someday," he said, and she thought *but we only have a few nights* before she banished the fleeting regret. Regretting was like counting down the days of a vacation before she'd even begun. She was lucky to have any time. She wouldn't waste it anticipating the end. Instead, she turned her head, giving him a small smile that was neither a yes nor a no. Let him figure it out.

He fisted her ponytail, drawing her head back and exposing the curve of her throat. "How rough?"

Heat rushed through her. Just hard enough that tomorrow she'd feel where he'd been inside her. She wanted him to mark her, to leave the faintest of scratches on her skin from his face because he was bigger and tougher than she, and then she could hold the reminder close for the rest of her time here on the island.

"Just rough enough." Those weren't good directions. She hadn't been specific. "I want to *see* you on my body tomorrow. I want to know, when I look at myself in the mirror, where you've touched me. I want to feel it everywhere."

He tugged her ponytail to the left, angling her head so he could kiss her. The position was awkward, forcing her to rise up on her toes to fit her mouth to his. It left her off-balance, trusting him with her weight.

"Laney?"

"Yeah?" How could she feel so out of control and yet connected with him? He hadn't even stuck his penis inside her yet, but she was hyper-aware of his body pinning hers. She dug her nails into the wall where he'd positioned them, using the small bite of rough plaster against her fingertips to ground herself.

"I can pretty much guarantee I'm not going to be gentle."

"Okay." That was her voice, breathless and needy.

"But I'm also going to make you feel good," he promised.

Saying something felt right, but she couldn't get the words out.

"Shhh." As if he knew she couldn't think, talk and feel at the same time. Or rather she could, but she'd rather not. He stretched her arms higher over her head. "Remember. Leave them there."

He was telling, not asking for permission. She nodded, anyway.

The rasp of his zipper coming down made her hotter. She wanted him to ram himself into her, to part her body with his and make her accommodate him. He'd do dirty things to her and then she'd do them to him because tit for tat was only fair, and his body drove her to crazy-good heights.

"Hurry up," she said, the words escaping her before she could bite them back.

He leaned in, giving her his full weight, his dick nestled against her butt. Her cheeks parted beneath the cotton of her shorts to accommodate him.

"Who's in charge?" He wanted to make his point, the answer clear, but that was part of the game, wasn't it? She ached deep between her thighs. He'd give it to her good.

When she didn't answer right away, because she wanted to see what he'd do, he dragged his penis up her butt and then back down again. His hand tangled in her hair, a heavy weight, as if he wasn't ever letting go.

"Laney." The stern warning in his voice deepened the ache.

"You are," she gasped.

She'd given him the words, now he had to give her what *she* wanted, right? Instead of sinking himself inside her body, however, he tugged down her tank top and the soft cup of her bra. He rubbed her nipples with the pad of his thumb while he twisted her head back and kissed her again. The rough stroke of his tongue taking her mouth matched the flick of his callused thumb and forefinger over her nipple. Then he plucked, hard, and she arched back into him with a cry.

"You have any idea how much I like that sound? Makes me want to kiss you and suck you, run my hands and my mouth over you until you come."

Yes, please. When she tried to angle her head so she could kiss him, he halted her with a hand in her hair.

"Nuh-uh. Hold still." A wave of heat followed the prickle against her scalp as she reached the end of her new leash.

When he rested his hand on the front of her shorts, she squirmed before she could stop herself. Her whole world focused on that hard hand cupping her. Her heartbeat banged in her ears, her breathing hitching and picking up speed.

"You can't get away," he growled, his voice low and authoritative. "And I'm taking what I want because you said I could."

His hand cradled her through the cotton, pressing in so there was no mistaking his intentions. No foreplay, no pretty words. He just dragged his fingers up, shoved them down the waistband of her shorts and underneath her panties, and all she could do was feel and trust him. He fingered her slick folds, parting her swollen flesh so he could push inside her.

She moaned.

He pumped in and out of her, his hand bumping against her panties. The tug of the cotton reminded her she was dressed and up against the wall.

His booted foot—oh, God, she loved his boots—kicked her legs wider. Her clit throbbed against his fingers as he pumped her with his hand. He gave her more, a second finger joining the first. Fuller, better, harder, the firm pressure made her head swim. The slick sounds filled the room, impossible to ignore, and heat seared through her. She was stretched around him, helpless to do anything but ride his hand and take him deep.

He lowered his mouth to her ear. "You could come just like this."

Maybe. But she was greedy and she wanted more. If she was *taking* what she wanted tonight, she was nowhere near done. She wanted more than ten minutes. But that was a guy for you. Kiss for so many minutes. Rub her breasts, snap on a condom and get down to business.

He backed off slightly. She felt a flash of disappointment—was he done *already*?—but then he was yanking her shorts and her panties down her legs, cool air brushing against her sweat-slicked skin. "Step out."

She did, pushing her shorts to one side with her foot. Hesitated.

"You want to pick them up and fold them, don't you?" Amusement colored his voice and so what if she did? Liking things to be organized wasn't a crime.

"Live dangerously, because I can't wait another minute to be inside you." His hot breath brushed against her ear and she swallowed another moan. She kicked her panties to the side and waited. Since this was her fantasy that put him in the driver's seat, the anticipation trickled through her like a heady aphrodisiac. Gray was one delicious surprise after another and just imagining what he might do next made her wetter.

"Good girl. Now hands over your head, up against the wall."

An answering urgency swept through her. She leaned back into the wall. They were so close that their bodies almost touched, yet inches of space remained between them. Stretching her arms up over her head, she arched her back slightly until her nipples grazed the front of his T-shirt and she was all laid out for him.

"I've got to feel you." He hauled his T-shirt over his head, tossing it behind him. Then he pulled her toward him until her nipples came into contact with his bare chest, and she felt the unexpected kiss of dog tags against her heated skin. *Soldier.*

Reaching between them, he shoved his pants down, and she curled her toes into the cool tile of the floor. *Hurry.*

Pinned up against the wall, the rough plaster rubbed against her bare skin, the hard surface strangely titil-

lating. He was fully dressed except for where he'd unzipped and bared himself, while she was naked from
the waist down, her bra pushed beneath her breasts. It
should have felt awkward, because she'd never been so
intensely aware of her nakedness. And she did feel exposed, confined...*sexy.*

Even the snap of the condom was exhilarating. God,
he was gorgeous and in a hurry and every bit as hot for
her as she was for him.

He stepped between her legs. "Straddle me."

She wasn't sure what he meant, but it didn't matter.
His hands found her hips, guiding her, and she let him
take over. He tugged and she slid down the wall, the
coarse prickle against her skin making her hotter. Then
he spread her bare thighs over his, his cargo pants teasing her. He opened her up with his thumbs, breaching
her folds. The fierce stab of pleasure followed the first
small throb from her clit.

Off balance, she wasn't sure what to do. "I need something to hold on to."

Before he could answer—*hello*, it was her fantasy
night, after all—she moved her hands down, gripping his
biceps. The muscles in his arms tightened and bunched.
She could feel the leashed power as he readied himself.

He cupped her butt with his hands, lifting her up.

"Ready?" He pressed her into the wall with barely
bridled aggression.

"Now," she demanded, squeezing his arms. *Oh, God,
yes.*

He bent his knees and pushed the thick head of his
cock inside her. And kept on coming. God. He was huge.
He sank into her, part rough, part tender, holding nothing back until he was sealed against her. The latex ring

of the condom stung against her opening, a scintillating sensation she couldn't get enough of. She rocked against him, working him inside, and then he thrust a little bit higher. *Harder.* A bright starburst of pleasure exploded behind her eyes as her clit slammed into him.

He lifted her, then dragged her back down, hammering into her with long, fast strokes that had her back arching with the sheer pleasure of it. Thinking? Impossible. Up, then down, he worked her on his dick as he thrust inside her. She dragged her hands up his arms, flattening her palms against his cheeks until she felt the rasp of stubble against her skin. The fierce look on his face was an even bigger turn-on. He made her feel as if she was the only woman in the world.

She wanted to remember this moment, to freeze it and tuck it away so she could pull it out later and relive it. This was their first time, a fantasy time *she'd* stolen, just for her. Whatever happened later, she had these memories of Gray going crazy for her. This was a dream, a wish she hadn't quite been able to put into words, and now it was a reality.

How did it feel to *him*? she wondered.

But then he thrust again and she lost her mind in the sensations, lost herself to the delicious push-pull of him moving inside her and opening her up. She groaned. He thrust, two, three, four times, his breathing harsh and controlled, and she could feel the immense power in his body as he held her up, angling her for his next stroke.

"I may not—" She was slow to orgasm. It took her a long time. Plus, she wasn't a featherweight. How long could he realistically hold her up? "I take a long time to come."

She waited for Gray to promise she'd come fast because he was *that* good, but he surprised her again. He nipped her lower lip hard, then laved the small sting.

"We don't have any time limits. We're doing this your way, so you come whenever you want or I'm not doing it right."

Then he slammed his mouth down on hers and kissed her. *Hard.* This time, she concentrated on him and his tongue, mirroring the push-pull of his cock in her. He devoured her mouth. Licking, sucking, biting. He was everywhere, and for a moment she panicked, not sure she could breathe. Then she found the rhythm, *their* rhythm, and kissed him back.

HE NEEDED TO get this right. Had to make it good for her. He knew, without Laney telling him, that she didn't let go often and so he wasn't going to screw this up. She'd asked for her fantasy and he'd deliver.

Laney liked things a little rough, so he fisted her hair with his hand, wrapping the silky brown strands around his fingers. She had pretty hair, all tidy and organized like her. He hadn't ever seen her with her hair down, not unless he got her that way. He didn't want to hurt her, just make her hot, so he angled her head back with a light yank, and she opened up to him. Her mouth ate his as if she couldn't get enough, her sexy whimpers getting him off. Her nails pricked his skin and damned if he didn't enjoy that, too. She'd marked him.

He pushed in hard.

She rewarded him with another husky moan.

He pushed her legs wider apart, forcing her thighs open with his. She was gonna ache in the morning, but she'd told him she liked that. She wanted to know where he'd been, wanted to feel him on every inch of her skin.

He could do that, too. Drawing her arms up over her head, he pinned her wrists with one hand. She moaned again and he pulled back, shoving into her until he was buried balls-deep.

"I'm not going slow."

"Good." She gasped the word. Another sign he was getting this right.

Give her fair warning. "I'm not done until the only thing you're screaming is my name."

"Cocky bastard." She didn't sound as if she minded.

He leaned in, pressing her into the wall. "You still want to pretend? Maybe that I've got you up against the wall behind the biker bar and we're doing it hard and quick, because anyone could come walking out. Some guy going for a smoke and he gets an eyeful. You think he'd enjoy watching you?"

Her nails dug deeper, her pussy clenching and squeezing every inch of his dick. He'd give almost anything to be buried in her without the latex, skin to skin.

He wanted to draw this out, to make them both wait to come, because this was their first time and possibly their only. She hadn't put a time limit on her fantasy, but she was only here on the island for a few days, and he was only here until he'd tagged and bagged Marcos. It didn't seem like anywhere near enough time, not now that she'd allowed him in.

He pulled out, pushed back in. Four, five, six deep thrusts that buried him all the way and sent her arching up toward him. Cupping her ass, he held her in place as he drove into her. He pounded into her, finding a fast, fierce rhythm that banged her into the wall, sealing them together.

"Keep your hands there," he growled, releasing her wrists.

Reaching between them, he thrummed her clit. Her sweet spot was hard and bursting beneath his thumb. She chanted his name in his ear, almost loud enough to be heard if anyone walked by. He liked that. He could take her outside, onto the beach maybe, and pound into her. Let her feel the excitement of doing it where some-one might catch her in the act.

"You're fucking perfect." He meant the words, too, and that scared him.

Shut up. He kissed her because he wasn't sure what might come out of his mouth and more to shut himself up than her. Plus, talking wasn't happening anymore. Her body clung to his, squeezing his dick in a greedy grip. The pleasure hit him out of nowhere, pleasure with a side of something else. Satisfaction, possession, who-the-hell-knew-what, because she dropped her hands from the wall and linked them around his neck.

"Gray." She whispered his name, and the heartfelt shudder was better than any scream he'd heard. Quiet satisfaction tore through him as she angled down toward him and she came, just like that, her eyes drifting shut. He wanted to know what she saw, what she was thinking of. Him, he hoped. Her pussy squeezed him and there was no holding off his own release. Instead, he buried his face against her throat, coming undone with her.

7

HOLY…WOW. THE MAN had turned her inside out. Rendered her boneless. He'd taken charge and stripped her of every ounce of self-control she possessed. She wasn't sure how she felt about that.

"That was fantastic," she said, because she felt the need to say something. To fill up the silence because he was staring at her, and she had no idea what he was thinking. She also felt more than a little ridiculous. She'd asked him for rough sex and, boy, had he delivered. The problem was that there was absolutely no graceful way to slide down the wall afterward and pretend she hadn't been shamelessly begging him to *give it to me harder* mere seconds ago.

Clothes. She needed clothes.

And space. Lots and lots of space.

"Tell me what worked for you," she said instead. He bent his knees and gently lowered her to the floor. One problem solved. *Treat this like any other operation. Review what happened. Identify areas to improve.* "No. Wait. Hold that thought."

Donning some clothes seemed prudent before they

started dissecting sex acts. She padded into the bathroom to grab a robe for them both. The his-and-her matched set hanging on the wall no longer seemed like a reminder of the love life she didn't have. Holy moly. What happened next now that the hot, spontaneous vacation hookup part of their evening was over? Because she wasn't ready to go to sleep—or to say goodbye to Gray.

Instead, she was recharged and full of energy. If the regrets hit tomorrow, she'd deal with them then. She liked the new Laney Parker, the woman who wasn't afraid to drag a sexy stranger into her bungalow and let him have his wicked way with her. She could worry about life and unemployment later. Or whether Gray intended to spend the night or not.

Don't overthink this. She snatched the robes from their matching hooks in the bathroom and slid into hers. Damn it. Should she tie the sash? Sashay back on out into the bedroom half-naked and give Gray ideas about doing it again? Find a pair of silky panties and slip into them? Really, she had no idea how other women handled this. When she walked out, tying the robe closed, he lounged on the bed. His new position gave her an awesome view of his big, powerful body. Not for the first time, she wondered what a masseuse had to do in his spare time to get that kind of physique. He'd zipped his pants back up, but hadn't bothered with his shirt. She took a good look, admiring the picture he made, even while the questions racked up. From the scars on his body, he'd been a frequent flyer at his local ER. In addition to the scars she'd already noticed on the beach, he had more scars on his rib cage and an exit wound on his right shoulder. Plus, he wore dog tags she'd noticed earlier.

She tried to keep the question in, but the words flew out, anyhow. "Where did you serve?"

He shook his head. "Doesn't matter."

It kind of did to her, part of that whole *get to know Gray better* plan. His battle scars said he'd been places, done things that he definitely hadn't shared. And, while it really wasn't any of her business, she was curious, and all that raw strength was attractive. He'd scooped her up effortlessly and held her against the wall. She wasn't a tiny woman, but he made her feel feminine and small in a way that was a delicious treat. Gray was chocolate cake after a diet. She couldn't do it often, but once in a while…it was okay to cheat and have things that were bad for her.

And he was very, very bad.

"Laney." He ground out her name. She might have forgotten positively everything in his arms—right down to her surroundings and her dignity—but she knew her own name, so she ignored him.

She perched on the edge of the bed and crossed one leg over the other. "If you won't tell me about your scars, give me the evening's highlights."

"Is this post-mortem a doctor thing?" He rolled onto his side, looking at her, and she could *hear* the lazy amusement coloring his voice. He thought she was being funny. He reached out a hand and curved his fingers around her thigh. She should have looked for those panties. "Lie down."

"Tell me what I didn't get one hundred percent right. I'm serious." She swung her feet up onto the bed and scooted toward him. She should probably get up and wash her feet first so she didn't get sand or something worse on the duvet. Why did hotels always choose white? It was so impractical.

He stroked his fingers over her thigh, nudging the robe out of the way. She made a face and flicked his fingers. Another inch and she'd forget her talking points. "Start talking."

He sighed. "You were perfect."

"Right." He looked serious…she'd give him that.

He tugged on the end of her sash. "Did you hear me complaining?"

"I'm not asking for complaints. I'm asking for feedback." Complaints were personal, him blowing off frustration or unhappiness, while feedback was actionable. Something she could fix or improve on.

"Uh-huh." He parted the front of her robe and trailed a hand over her waist, clearly not interested in a vocabulary lesson.

"I want to know." She was the best doctor in the ER chute, and she'd managed that by studying hard and learning from her mistakes. Failure wasn't an option. Why shouldn't sex be the same?

"Why do you care if I have the best time of my life in bed with you, as long as you enjoy the hell out of it?" Genuine curiosity replaced amusement in his voice.

She pointed to his groin. "Biology requires a certain level of participation from you."

"It still doesn't have to be the best hard-on of my life."

"Can you tell the difference between erections?" That had to be a safe topic.

He gave her a look. "Can you tell a difference between your orgasms?"

Absolutely. Maybe they needed to forget this whole conversation, however, because she had no intention of telling him that tonight's orgasm had been hands down the best of her life. He didn't need to know just how much he affected her, did he?

"Come here." He tugged her sash again.

"I have the munchies. No more sex until I've been fed. Do you want room service?"

He quirked a brow. "Do you want the entire resort to know I'm here?"

Right. She didn't think he'd hide in the bathroom while the room service guy delivered. She couldn't tell from his expression if he'd mind everyone knowing about them or not. How many of the island's employees hooked up with the guests? Some, but not enough, she decided. Chances were, he didn't want to advertise their hookup.

She shrugged and headed for the tiny fridge. "I'm voting for instant gratification. Let's hit up the minibar."

"That's not a meal."

She looked over her shoulder and grinned at him. "How do you know what I've got in my minibar?"

"Are you hiding a steak in there? Because a meal definitely includes protein."

She made a face, even though she knew he couldn't see it. What was it with men and beef? "Prepare for disappointment."

The bed creaked as he resettled himself. Apparently, he wasn't of the bang-her-and-leave school of thought. She sighed. He was too tempting. Maybe it *would* be better if he hightailed it for the door.

"Nothing about you could disappoint."

His words were the cherry on a really great Gray sundae. She was tempted to turn around so she could see his face, but maybe it had been a throwaway line. So looking would be a mistake and wouldn't be cool. To keep herself busy and her mind off sexy compliments, she opened the fridge and rifled through its overpriced contents. No steak, but she did have two mini bottles of champagne. She turned around, waving her prizes.

"Woo-hoo! We win."

He eyed the tiny bottles in her hand. "I'm not much of a drinking man."

She hadn't pegged him for a health-kick guy, but whatever. "That must come with the spa job."

He snorted. "That comes with childhood territory. I've seen too many people turn into idiots once they'd pounded a few beers."

No alcohol. Check. She grabbed him a bottled water instead, the sparkling kind with an Italian name and fancy glass bottle. That probably wasn't his thing, either, but the minibar had limited options.

"No steak," she said with a smirk. She'd brought her own stuff and shoved it inside the minibar on top of the resort's overpriced offerings. She needed healthy snacks in her life, thank you very much. She'd brought a Japanese trail mix with seaweed, nuts and dried fish. Since dried fish wasn't everybody's thing, she grabbed a handful of more mainstream offerings, went back to the bed and dropped the impromptu picnic onto the duvet. "Dig in."

He eyed Snack Mountain with some doubt, prodding her Japanese mix dubiously. "Is that even edible?"

She dropped onto the bed beside him. "It has omegas. Omegas are good for you."

He shuddered. "Give me chocolate any day. Dried fish is the kind of shit you eat after the apocalypse hit and the survivors have looted all the good stuff from the gas station."

"Cheerful." She popped another handful into her mouth.

Reaching over, he grabbed the Snickers bar from her stash. "This, on the other hand, is a snack. A *good* one."

"If you say so." Too much sugar for her.

"Are you sure you're a girl?" He eyed her suspiciously as he peeled back the wrapper and proceeded to devour her candy.

"You would know."

"True." He polished off the candy bar and reached for a second one.

Picnicking on the bed was strangely intimate and almost as much fun as the sex. Well, not really, but it added a side of sweet to her savory. Gray was good company. He asked her about working as a trauma surgeon and what it was like living in San Francisco. She couldn't help but notice, though, that he didn't volunteer any information about himself. Granted, she hadn't asked for his résumé before she'd jumped his bones, but there had to be a story that brought this man to this place. Whatever it was, he wasn't in a sharing mood.

"Are you done eating?" He set his bottled water on the bedside table.

Deflection? Or deliciously horny intentions? Because she could be done with the right incentive.

She looked at her champagne bottle. Definitely empty. So…yes? She set it down.

"Why? What did you have in mind?"

She landed on her back. Damn, she hadn't even heard him move, but she saw him now as he swung himself over her.

"Because I'm not done with you yet," he said, his hands coming down on the bed on either side of her face, his thumbs stroking over her cheeks like he couldn't get enough of her. And...just like that, she lost interest in snacks. "I'm a fast learner. Want to see what else I think you'd like?"

Yeah, she absolutely did. Thank God she'd stocked up on condoms, because it appeared her fantasy night wasn't over yet.

8

FANTASY ISLAND HAD one restaurant, a fancy seaside bistro perched on wooden piers over the calm lagoon. The establishment had a palapa roof, but was otherwise open to take advantage of the sea air and breezes. Since the staff baited the waters regularly, it also came with a couple of lazy sharks and schools of brightly colored tropical fish waiting for their next handout. The wildlife was good, although the white tablecloths and four-hundred-piece tableware setting were definitely out of Laney's league. She was more of a spork kind of gal. She survived on sandwiches and coffee from the hospital vending machine, or carnitas from the taco truck if it was Friday.

Had survived, she reminded herself. That job was gone.

Ashley high-fived her as soon as she sat down at the table. "You got some."

Maddie made a face. Her nose was peeling from a recent sunburn. "That has to be one of the crudest phrases ever."

The waiter slid a tray of appetizers in front of them.

All-inclusive, she reminded herself. *Prepaid.* She should live it up before she had to go back to the real world and microwaved Lean Cuisine meals. Not that there was anything wrong with frozen dinners, but the extra five thousand calories in the stuffed mushrooms staring up at her begged her to indulge. And it wasn't willpower week.

Ashley didn't look concerned about her word choice as she forked up a large mouthful of salad greens. "Look at her face and tell me I'm wrong. She's rocking the post-coital glow look. Do you want me to dress it up?"

What was she supposed to say? Because right now what she felt was a combination of awkward and excited. Holy smokes, she'd actually done it. She'd picked a fantasy and made it come true with a hot stranger. Just remembering last night, she wanted to run back to the massage cabanas or employee housing, find Gray and do it all over again. Which she could. If she wanted to.

Right?

The deal hadn't *necessarily* been for one night only. Seeing Gray again, both naked and fully clothed, wasn't off the table. She wanted to kiss him, touch him, learn what had brought him to this island.

Okay. She also wanted to have sex with him. Lots and lots of sex, followed by the rest of the night curled up in bed. Gray had stayed the night, not slipping out until the sun was about to come up, and it turned out the man was as good at snuggling as he was at sex.

Maddie pointed a fork at her. "Crappy phrasing aside, was he any good?"

Thank God for the champagne that had magically materialized in her glass. "Yes."

Ashley bit into a mushroom with a groan of pleasure. "On a scale of one to ten, rate him. Would you do him again?"

Wait. Why was that even a question?

"The blush says it all," Ashley observed, then stared down at her empty plate. "I would kill for a drive-through burger and fries."

"Fast food is terrible for your arteries."

"But it tastes good, Doctor Sexy, and it fills me up."

Laney shrugged. "Still going to kill you."

"Point taken. Was it kinky?"

Maddie elbowed Ashley. "Do *you* have sweet fantasies?"

Ashley grinned. "No comment. I bet she let him tie her up."

Maddie looked thoughtful. "Or *she* tied *him* up."

Oh. My. God. Why had she thought she wanted girlfriends? And why did they always have to discuss her sex life over food? The calorie guilt was bad enough. "Sorry to disappoint you, but no rope was involved."

"Bummer. Gray seems like a take-charge kind of guy." Ashley flagged the waiter down and proceeded to order what sounded like half a cow and ketchup.

Madeline waved her champagne flute at her friend. "How would you know, hotshot? I haven't seen you hanging around the massage cabanas. You're judging the man by his appearance."

Which was admittedly gorgeous. Laney could almost have been satisfied just looking at Gray. He was big, he was ripped and he had no problem with being naked. Lucky her, she got to look *and* touch.

Ashley wasn't conceding. "Are you telling me looks are deceiving?"

"She has a point," Laney told Maddie. Gray's performance in bed definitely lived up to the promise of his big, sexy body.

"So he's bossy in the bedroom and you enjoy that."

Silence was definitely her better choice. Condemning, but wiser.

"When do you see him again?" Maddie asked.

She shrugged. "I don't know. We didn't talk about that. It was kind of a one-time hookup thing."

"Do him again," Ashley urged.

Maddie squeaked in embarrassment, fake-fanning her face with her napkin. "Give her some time to make up her own mind."

"What?" Ashley grinned. "It's like having seconds on dessert. It's vacation, so it's definitely allowed. Plus, if she waits too long, someone else may cut her in line and take all the good chocolate on the dessert buffet."

"Do you know what she's talking about?" Maddie demanded. "Because I know she's talking about sex, but I've lost track of the details."

"Sex. Chocolate. Take your pick."

"I'm not picking anything," Maddie grumbled. "That's my problem right there. I just blog about it secondhand for others to read about."

Ashley, however, clearly had no intention of stopping. And note to self: *make sure secret vacation sexcapades don't end up on a blog somewhere.* "Is he into bondage? Does he do the kinky stuff?"

"TMI." Maddie closed her eyes briefly. "This is the kind of conversation that gets recorded and played back on daytime television. Just saying."

"We're not playing bondage games," Laney said firmly. *Yet.* Hands didn't count. They needed ropes to qualify as seriously kinky.

"Just wait until your second date," Ashley said, smiling broadly.

Laney didn't need Gray to take charge outside the bedroom, and she wasn't in the market for happily-ever-after—been there, done that, got the credit card bill. But this was supposed to be *her* fantasy, after all. She'd always been the person in control and in the driver's seat of her heart, body and sexual desires, so indulging in some naughty role play was strangely seductive. She didn't have to worry about whether or not he was happy and enjoying himself—all she had to worry about was herself.

She also had positively no self-control around the man. He showed up, gave a few macho commands and she happily dropped her panties. On the other hand, having the hottest, dirtiest sex of her admittedly vanilla life hadn't made him open up or cuddle her close, or do any of the other relationship things she was used to.

Yep. That definitely worked for her.

Maddie tapped her fingers against the tablecloth, trying to get her attention. "Do you have plans to see him again?"

"Not yet."

The waiter returned with a load of steak, fries, ice cream and what had to be half a chocolate cake. Ashley might have the manners of a trucker, but she sure knew how to order. She was also bossy as hell, because she banged a spoon against her water glass to get their attention.

"Let's discuss next steps in Plan To Get Laney Laid."

"We could plan *your* love life, instead."

Ashley shook her head. "Uh-uh. Maddie's next."

Madeline groaned. "I'm a lost cause. Focus on Laney."

Ashley pulled a set of laminated cards out of her

beach bag and slapped them down onto the table. "Research time. I've brought the list of possibilities."

The menu didn't look like anything out of the ordinary. It was maybe six pages of drink names, with the occasional picture of something pink and fruity. Or in a coconut. Laney strained to find something erotic about it, but it was just a list of alcoholic beverages. Some of them with ice cream. Yum. She pulled it over and started flipping through it. If orgasms weren't happening, ice cream was next on her list.

A Good Night Kiss	*Leather and Lace*
A Tender Touch	*Much Fuss for the Conquering Hero*
All Night Long	*Seduction on the Rocks*
Black Leather Whip	*See You in the Morning*
Cowboy Up	*Sex on the Beach*
Kinky Sex	*Sex with the Bartender*
Kiss-in-the-Dark	*Slow Comfortable Screw*

Okay. Some of the options seemed anatomically impossible, while others were clearly optimistic. *Seduction on the Rocks*, for instance, was clearly a fantasy that no one in her right mind would reenact. The slow, comfortable screw, however, had promise. Lots of sexy Gray promise. *Wait.* She tore her gaze away from the menu.

"How do you know this really isn't just a list of drinks?" Because it *sure* looked like a list, even if every single name had something to do with sex. Maybe the bartender had a dirty mind. Or really, really liked laughing his butt off when somebody ordered a—she flipped the page and squinted—*Slippery Nipple*. She wanted to feel sexy, not ridiculous.

Maddie scooted closer and stabbed a drink with her finger. "I had this one last night. Believe me, no orgasms were involved. Marketing hype is like penis hype—all words, no action."

Since Ashley was the one who had first brought up the drinks menu, that made her the expert. "So how do you know it works?"

Maddie grinned. "Have you tried it? And, if so, which drink do you recommend?"

Ashley tapped the side of her nose. "Not telling. And I have inside sources. The question really is—does Laney start at the top and work her way down, or just pick her favorites?"

KICKING THE RADIO would be a stupid move. Gray needed the radio. He simply hadn't expected the bad news the guy on the other end had delivered. The bad news fit the incoming crappy weather to a tee. A slow-moving storm had blown up about an hour ago, and now rain was pounding the island, the drops practically flying sideways. The night was perfect for cozying up to a bar—or waking up Laney and getting her going all over again. Instead, he was stuck out here in a seriously damp patch of jungle, rainwater dripping off his tent while the local mosquito population circled him as if he was an all-you-can-eat buffet.

Good thing he loved his job.

"You cannot be serious." Levi cursed and started disassembling his M16. Not that the gun needed cleaning, but the man had energy to burn and hated sitting still. "They can't do that to us."

Gray scoffed. "When's the last time we had a choice about the mission timeline?"

Levi cursed again. His shooter's position on the time change was crystal clear.

"Marcos's advance team lands in three hours." Mason said the words out loud, as if verbalizing the FUBAR situation would make it better.

"That's the new plan. Our target is either itching to get his tropical relaxation on or he's decided that *unpredictable* is the new *safe*." Gray fell back on the stack of duffel bags. Their camp was neat and orderly, despite their prime location in the jungle. Thunder boomed, low and close, the downpour on their canvas roof dancing at tango speed. He'd spent more than a few months concealed in similar patches of wet, mosquito-infested jungles, waiting out a target.

But somehow, it sucked worse, knowing Laney was tucked up in her bungalow, all sweet and warm. He'd much rather be there than here, and that was a problem. There was no solving it now, however, so he forced himself to focus on his present reality: that his ass was parked in a tent in a SEAL camp.

Some of the guys liked to create a little piece of home inside their tents, with photos and pictures, as if those pieces of paper were windows into the normal goings-on thousands of miles away. Or a reminder of what they were fighting for. He'd never needed that. Give him a bedroll and his weapons bag and he was good.

Nope. The two-thousand-dollar-a-night luxury bungalows two clicks away weren't his thing. He wasn't a fancy kind of guy. He liked beer, bikes and camping. Laney Parker, on the other hand, was the kind of woman who deserved the finer things in life. Not that she was a prima donna or demanded five-star treatment, but she had a classiness about her that made him want to give her the best life could offer. For a couple of days only, he reminded himself. She wasn't interested in keeping him, and he *definitely* didn't want her anywhere near Marcos and his muscle.

Levi set down the first rifle and reached for a second. "We're certain Marcos is moving early?"

"Positive. Our inside guy confirmed it." The man had taken an enormous risk to get that intel out to them fast. Gray appreciated it. Having Marcos's advance team show up unannounced wouldn't have been good. He was already walking a tightrope between baiting the trap sufficiently for Marcos and keeping the civvies at ground zero safe.

"We need to insert the second SEAL team ASAP," he continued.

The original plan had called for Gray's team to infiltrate the resort staff and lay the groundwork for a second team that would come in later to provide backup. The insert had to be quick. Stealthy was also a definite requirement. The second team was scheduled to drop from two helos that would come in low over the bay behind their campsite in case Marcos had eyes on the ground, which was highly likely. Bringing the helos in and hitting the pause button over the beach would give the guys a narrow window to fast rope down to the ground. Team unloaded, the helos would head back to the Navy tanker waiting in international waters. Gray needed to be able to handle the situation with the utmost skill and prowess. This was his team and his guys on the line.

"We meet and greet with the second SEAL team, then we lay up and wait for Marcos's advance team. His guys are coming in early, but resort staff is up at dark o'clock. Our asses are going to be saved by the shit weather—the early morning yoga and jogging crazies aren't going to be on the beach. If we do it fast, we should be clear before anyone notices."

As much as he wanted to get Laney's butt off the island immediately, it simply wasn't possible, and only part of his concern was due to the fact that she was a civilian who hadn't signed up to be part of a covert military operation. He didn't want to see her get hurt. She should be just another piece in the chess game of his mission, a convenient prop for his undercover role, but she wasn't. He had to admit that much to himself. She was something—*someone*—more. Sex had definitely been a bad idea.

Levi looked over at him. "Ready to get the party started?"

Anything to get him out of his head. "Let's roll."

It took over an hour to cross the island to the designated landing zone. It would have been quicker to cut through the resort, but riskier. So they'd gone the long way, skirting the pathways in a long, slow crawl through the jungle as they made for the beach. They had to run blind because Marcos could have eyes on the water and light would give them away. There was no way a casual tourist was running around in this kind of rain in the middle of the night.

Dark-oh-hundred and raining. Some days his job sucked. There was definitely no getting a civilian chopper off the ground now. The resort's seaplane might have been an option, but the plane didn't handle best under gusty conditions, and that was what they were looking at now. So all he needed to do was to keep any firefight away from the guest bungalows.

The bay didn't look quite so picturesque when they reached it. The rain tore up the lagoon and dripped off the palm trees. Of course it was where he'd watched Laney run, so his beach fantasy came back with a vengeance. But he knew better than anyone that erections and missions didn't go together. Levi took position on Gray's left, while Mason moved out in front, Sam and Remy heading silently east and disappearing into the surf. They'd be waiting under the pier when the Zodiacs came in. The ocean was mad as hell tonight, the surf churning relentlessly up onto the wet sand. The Black Hawk swept in over the lagoon right on schedule, lights off, until it hovered over the beach.

Mason eyed the choppy lagoon. "Those boys better hope they don't miss and fall in."

"Choices." Levi tapped his finger against his teeth. "Skewer your ass on a coral head or serve as a shark's late-evening snack."

Sharks were a potential issue at night, although the lagoon was sheltered. Bull sharks in particular were night feeders, and it was possible to run into one even in these shallower waters. The low number of recorded shark attacks made it a low-risk proposition, however, and Levi knew that. He was just having fun with them.

"Maybe sharks don't like SEAL sushi." Gray hunkered down to wait as the rest of his team disappeared into the dark.

"Five bucks says we find out." Levi flashed him a grin, his teeth white against his face paint.

The chopper settled into a holding pattern, and the rope master tossed out one hundred fifty feet of fast rope. The rope bounced, smacking into the strip of wet sand where beach met ocean. According to the plan, they had ten minutes to unload and get the Black Hawk the hell out before they ran the risk of being spotted by the incoming Zodiacs.

Showtime. Salt, sand and the heavy, lush weight of the water-soaked jungle air made breathing difficult. Even after dark and in the pouring rain, it was still hotter than hell, and the full camo didn't help. Gray had water in his boots, and if he tipped his head back and opened his mouth, he ran the risk of waterboarding himself. Good times. At least he wasn't packing fifty pounds of gear like the incoming SEALs.

The deployment bags came out first, dropping from the open door and hitting the beach. Then the first SEAL swung his legs out the door, grabbed the rope and dropped. As soon as his boots hit, he ran for the jungle cover, a green blur in Gray's night-vision goggles. The team commander slid down the rope last, then the Black Hawk rose up and banked sharply, moving out and away in a quick blast of sand and water.

Gray checked the time as the other team leader loped across the sand to join him. They were on schedule. Twenty minutes to go-time, and the Zodiacs' arrival at the main dock, if Marcos's advance team didn't decide to shake their shit up. It was a mighty big *if.* Signaling for the other SEAL to follow, he headed toward the dock.

Marcos's advance team was playing it cool, pretending to be resort guests. They had to land on the helo pad or arrive at the dock to avoid arousing suspicion. The pad was set a half mile away from the resort to preserve the peace and quiet of the bungalows. Guests arriving by helicopter were then driven to the resort in jeeps or golf carts. Ashley's intel said the advance team was coming in by Zodiac. That meant there was a yacht cruising just offshore, hence the Black Hawk's stealth approach.

When they reached the dock, he signaled for a halt. The pier was too close to the guest bungalows for his liking. If they failed to contain Marcos's advance team, all hell could break loose. Still, Laney didn't know what was going down, he reminded himself. She wouldn't be wandering around and into danger. If he did his job right, she'd sleep through tonight and wake up in the morning none the wiser.

At sixty seconds to go-time, the familiar dark shape of a Zodiac hit the slot, driving through the channel, and rode the swells toward the beach. Marcos's men had dropped the boat from a fishing vessel several miles offshore. He scanned the Zodiac with his night-vision goggles, grabbing a quick head count. Six men. The expected number and no surprises. The SEALs from the second team would be moving into formation behind them as they closed on the dock. It should be straightforward, but Gray had had far too many missions go strange to tempt fate.

So far, so good, though.

The Zodiac bumped against the dock and resort "staff" moved out to greet the new arrivals, carrying trays of chilled juice and hot towels. Since using civilians was an unacceptable risk, the two men were actually undercover operatives. The plan was to avoid a shooting war, so he had two snipers up in the trees. His receiver crackled in his ear as the first of his shooters reported in. "I don't have a clear shot."

The SEALs kicked up out of the water, taking down their targets, and the two SEALs on the dock hit the ground as they palmed the weapons they'd concealed in their waistbands. And just like that, gunfire erupted. *Damn it.* Someone would hear the noise and investigate.

"Backup plan." Gray lunged out of the jungle, rifle up, running all out for the Zodiac. One hundred yards of sand, followed by another thirty feet of shallow water. It was remarkably similar to running through concrete. As his boots hit the water, the splash giving away any remaining element of surprise, he decided there was probably a market for a workout DVD like that. He aimed and squeezed off a round as heads turned in his direction. Unlike Marcos's advance team, his had a silencer.

A sharp stinging sensation in his side announced the unwelcome news that somebody on Marcos's side had both excellent aim and armor-piercing rounds. He gritted his teeth against the pain.

Well. Hell.

FANTASY ISLAND'S EMPLOYEE quarters were no military hospital with state-of-the-art equipment. The small single room housed a bed and a straight-back chair in addition to a sink and a mirrored medicine cabinet. Compared to the luxury bungalows dotting the beach, the room was positively spartan. Still, Gray was damned glad to see a bed even if lying down wasn't an option at the moment. Hitting the mattress could be his backup plan. He peeled off his equipment and then his T-shirt. The bullet had grazed his side, just below his rib cage, the worst of the potential damage averted by his body armor.

Patching up the damage was never fun.

The door opened and closed behind him. Since Mason

was standing watch out in the hallway, his incoming guest had to be an ally.

"If you bleed on the floor, you clean it up." The voice belonged to Sam, their field medic. Good times. Gray didn't get to bleed alone anymore.

Dropping the bloody T-shirt on the floor, he swabbed it around with his foot, ignoring Sam's bark of laughter. "Cleanup's a snap."

"Says you." Levi didn't move from his position leaning against the wall.

"How did you get shot?" Sam asked as he dropped his med kit on the bed. Too bad they couldn't fast-forward to the next part of the night.

"The usual way," he snorted. "Someone aimed and pulled the trigger. I failed to move in time."

"Lucky for you his aim was off." Sam patted the bed. "Sit. The doctor is in."

If he sat, he wouldn't get back up. He gripped the edge of the sink. "I'm good here."

"The medical equivalent of a drive-through. Excellent." Sam moved up behind him, snapping on a pair of latex gloves. "Are you planning on dying on me?"

"Not tonight," he gritted out. Even the most superficial bullet wounds hurt like a bitch. He always forgot how much.

"Good to know." Sam carefully prodded, and Gray's breath hissed out through his teeth. The key to dealing with an injury was to patch it up and ignore it. Too bad the *patching* part was so unpleasant.

"Slap a Band-Aid on it and call it good." The second SEAL team was moving Marcos's advance team to an American vessel as they spoke, and he wanted to keep an eye on the transfer.

Before Sam could answer—and undoubtedly protest—the door opened and closed again.

"Is this a goddamned party?" Gray knew the question came out more growl than not, but now he felt like a sideshow. He'd shake this off, but it would be easier if he were alone.

"If it is, it's the worst party I've ever been to." Ashley strode toward him and eyed Gray's side as if he was a painting in a freaking art gallery. Not that her camo and boots were opening-night attire, but Gray had a bad feeling he wasn't thinking clearly. "Wow. You need to move faster."

She looked at Sam. "How bad is it?"

He shrugged. "I'm a field medic. It looks fairly superficial to me, but we're in the tropics. The possibility for infection is high."

"I'm not pulling out." Tight timeline aside, he wasn't sending his unit in against Marcos alone. They needed every man. The advance team hadn't gone down easily, and security would be tighter around Marcos.

Ashley cursed. For a pretty girl, she sure had a potty mouth. It was no wonder she fit in so well with the SEAL unit. They weren't pretty, either.

"Laney's a doctor," she suggested. "Get her to fix you."

Laney was also a civilian. Under no circumstances was he dragging her into his operation.

"Not an option," he snapped. "Give me a shot of antibiotic and bandage up the damage. Think you can do that?"

Sam growled right back, but he also moved away and grabbed his bag and started sorting out supplies, which meant Gray got his way tonight.

Ashley wouldn't let it go. "Laney's a trauma surgeon.

She's one of the best there is, and you want Sam to patch you up, instead? No offense, Sam."

"None taken." The medic added a roll of gauze to his stack of supplies. The gauze was harmless. The scissors, however, were one more item in a pile of sharp, pointy objects Gray had no desire to examine too closely. This was going to hurt.

"She's a civilian." And that was certainly part of the truth.

Laney wasn't part of the SEAL unit. She didn't have combat training, and he wanted to keep her far, far away from Marcos and his goons. So, yeah, she was a doctor. And she had undoubtedly patched up far worse in the ER chutes, but he didn't want to be one more gunshot victim asking for help. Hell. He didn't ask for help period, plus, looking helpless in front of Laney was the last thing he ever wanted to do.

"She's a trauma surgeon," Ashley repeated. "She's seen worse, and if anyone can get you back up and running quickly, it's Laney."

"Laney stays out of this." He sucked in a breath, tightening his grip on the sink as Sam began to explore the wound.

"At least lie down." Ashley sounded impatient. "Do you have an aversion to mattresses, as well?"

Not at all. If he lay down, however, he wouldn't be getting back up in the near future. He'd also make one hell of a mess on the sheets and that would be harder to conceal.

"Sam's going to be quick." *Please God.* The medic did something that sent fire blazing through his side, and Gray started counting. Get to ten and then reassess. He could do that.

Sam grunted, focused on his work. "Take an aspirin. You'll live."

Good news, because hell would freeze over before he went knocking at Laney's door with this kind of trouble.

9

THE PERSISTENT SOUND of rain hammering the palm trees and then Laney's umbrella almost drowned out the sound of the ocean. According to the weather report that resort staff had slipped under her door last night, a small tropical storm had moved into the area for the next couple of days. Booking massages by the pool would be off-limits. The surrounding jungle was damp and wet, the early-morning sky dull.

The walk to the employee housing was a ten-minute exercise in second-guessing herself. The employees occupied a neat, two-story apartment building tucked behind a discreet screen of palm trees. A watery sun rose over the ocean, almost entirely concealed by the falling rain. Those people who compared tropical rain to drops of pineapple juice? They were dead wrong.

She spotted few lights on in the building. Please let Ashley be right about which room was Gray's. She had a second fantasy to try on him. So, if the mountain wouldn't come to Mohammed…she'd go to him. She liked walking in the rain, but cozying up in bed with Gray seemed like the better choice right now. Especially since the constant rain had soaked her running shoes and kicked mud up the back of her legs. Romantic. *Not*.

When she stepped into the hallway, however, a dark shadow moved to intercept her, and she tried to remember how to breathe. It was just one of the resort employees. Who apparently had a thing for camo gear in his off hours. He paired military-grade boots, BDU pants and a damp T-shirt stretched over his powerful chest. And…was that a gun?

"Can I help you with something?" The deep, smoky voice that came out of the darkness meant business. While the voice's owner waited for her answer, he angled his body between hers and the hallway, cutting off her view of the gun tucked in the waistband of his pants.

In some ways he reminded her of the gangbangers she'd patched up in the San Francisco ER. He wore the same easy confidence and animal-like awareness as the tattooed, low-rider men who'd prowled the inner-city streets, flashing gang signs and inking their allegiances into their skin. In other ways he resembled private security. He moved with lazy grace, as if it was simply a given he was bigger, badder and armed. *Dangerous*. She recognized the physical confidence of a man who knew he could take down anyone who got in his way. She posed no threat to him.

"I'm looking for Gray." She'd have bet this guy, whoever he was, knew about the two of them even before she spoke the words, and his nod confirmed her suspicions.

"I'll tell him you stopped by." He didn't move from his position in the middle of the hallway.

"No need. I'll tell him myself." She took a step forward, testing him. The man was built like a brick wall. There would be no getting through him.

"Gray's busy right now."

What the hell did that mean? It was practically dark o'clock and the spa wasn't open for business yet. She peered over the guy's shoulders—the man was roughly the size of an *ox*—and, sure enough, that was Gray's room right there. Her sneakers touched boots, her body very much in his personal space. And he didn't budge. Damn it.

"Who are you?" she demanded.

He gave her a half smile. "I'm Mason. I'm a cook."

No. He wasn't. A low groan reached her through the door. *Gray's* voice. She recognized the sound as easily as she recognized the rough note of pain, the smell of antiseptic and, beneath that, blood.

"Now would be a good time to leave." Mason nodded toward the exit. A black harness crisscrossed his chest, and a lethal-looking knife hung from his waist. Definitely not a cook.

Nothing on Fantasy Island was what it seemed. The resort was staffed by a group of rough, scarred men and Mason was packing? Any number of scenarios ran through her head, none of them good, but then a second groan issued from Gray's bedroom, abruptly cut off.

She swallowed. What was going on here? "I'm a doctor."

"Yeah." Mason curled his hands around her upper arms. Gently, as if he knew just how badly he could hurt her and he was being extra careful. Or maybe she was imagining things. She stared at the door, debating.

"You know what the Hippocratic Oath is?"

Mason stared down at her, eyes hooded. "I'm aware of it."

"That oath means you need to step aside and let me do my job. Whatever's wrong with Gray, I can fix him."

"Maybe." Mason looked thoughtful. That had to be a good sign, right? Because the man was almost as impassive as Gray. When he stepped aside, she made a beeline for Gray's door, throwing it open without knocking.

The door bounced off someone large and immovable. A second later a hard male body slammed her up against the wall and pinned her in place. Dimly she registered that she'd have bruises tomorrow, but adrenaline spiked, her body amping her up for fight or flight. Heart pounding, she fought to breathe, her fingers scrabbled at the powerful forearm across her throat. When that didn't work, she kicked out, and the man immediately immobilized her legs with one of his own.

"Levi. Put her down," someone snapped. Ashley's voice, but what would her new girlfriend be doing in Gray's room?

Levi dropped her feet to the ground and removed his forearm from her throat. He looked dubious, but at least breathing was now a possibility. She sucked in air for a moment, concentrating on not having a heart attack, and then shoved him out of the way. He let her. They both knew that, but it felt good.

"Explain." She snapped the one-word order to Ashley, but she was already moving toward the two men standing by the sink. The room was crowded with too many people for the limited space. She counted Ashley. The Neanderthal who'd pinned her. A second man. And Gray. Oh, my God. *Gray.*

Shirtless, Gray strangled the porcelain rim of the sink with his fingers. Blood streaked the bowl and his side. The unfamiliar man crouched beside him, the contents

of a medic's kit strewn across the bed. Her instincts—
and possibly her heart—demanded she rush across the
room and pull him close. Wrap him up in her arms and
promise everything was going to be okay.

Not helpful.

Drawing on years of training, she forced herself to
perform a quick visual assessment of the wound while
she leaned over the sink, soaping up because clearly
Gray needed a doctor and not a girlfriend. From here,
she could see a long, bloody crease in his side, but without an obvious entrance or exit wound. There was also
no visible powder stippling, no telltale spray of gun-
powder residue around the injury. He'd likely been fully
clothed when he'd been shot, with more than one layer
between him and the bullet. He was upright, indicating
he'd walked to the room.

"Tell me what we've got." She grabbed his wrist, checking his pulse while she waited for Gray's answer. His heart
rate was elevated, but that was to be expected.

"Go back to your room," he gritted out.

She ignored him. Typical male. Either he'd injured
himself doing something stupid or—more likely, from
the looks of his audience—something illegal and dangerous. He didn't want her to witness this? Too bad.

She performed a more detailed head-to-toe assessment. Since his pants had no visible tears, his injuries
were likely limited to the one bullet wound. It could
have been worse than what looked to be a bad graze.
She grabbed the paper towel Ashley held out and dried
her hands off.

"I'm a doctor. Switch," she ordered.

The guy performing first aid hesitated. "Sam Nale.
Combat medic."

She almost snarled at him, but then her training took over. This wasn't Gray. It was a gunshot victim.

"Step out and let me take over." Switching places with the medic, she got her first closer look at the injury. "Bullet creased the left side. Close range. Do you have a local anesthetic?"

Sam nodded. "I've got a regional."

"Shoot him up and I'll finish cleaning it out before I stitch it up."

"No drugs," Gray gritted out. "This is—"

"Don't say it's just a scratch," she said. "Because try walking around with an open wound in the tropics and see what happens. I guarantee you won't enjoy it."

He shut up, then Ashley snorted. "He's a guy. You can cut his leg off and he'll still say he's fine."

She probed the injury carefully. "Do you know the make of gun?"

"Why?" Levi leaned in, watching her more closely than a first-time dad at a birth as she began to irrigate the wound. Gray's breath hissed through his teeth and she laid a gentle, calming hand on his back.

"Professional curiosity? It could also be because I'm weighing the odds of the bullet having fragmented. In which case, I'm going to have to do some digging to make sure we're completely clean here."

Ashley exchanged looks with Levi. Clearly deciding how much to share, but that was okay. Sutures, she decided, finally satisfied the raw crease in Gray's side was as clean as she could get it. He also needed a course of antibiotics.

"A semiautomatic." Gray didn't flinch as she set the first stitch.

She whistled. "That's not standard resort wear."

"Nope." He didn't volunteer any more information, though.

"You might as well tell her," Ashley said from the bed.

"Or we can assume that I've already correctly guessed you're not a masseuse." She taped the dressing over the wound site.

"It's not all I am."

Objectively, she'd known the moment she walked into his room that he'd been keeping secrets. Apparently, practice didn't make the familiar, sick sense of betrayal any easier to swallow, though. Harlan had tried various excuses for his infidelity. Eventually, he'd settled on the *it was just a fantasy* story. On the one hand, Gray didn't owe her anything. She hadn't needed to know that the US Military was at work on Fantasy Island. On the other hand, she'd had *every* right to know that her lover wasn't who she thought he was.

"Don't split hairs with me."

"I'm also SEAL Lieutenant Commander Gray Jackson."

Part of her, the part that wasn't busy being Doctor Laney Parker, realized she hadn't known his last name. She'd had sex with this man without knowing his name. She wasn't sure what that said about her, but that was something to worry about later. When he *wasn't* bleeding. "You're here on an operation." It explained a lot.

"I can't tell you the details."

"Then give me the big picture." Surely he owed her that much for the patch job.

"We got word that Fantasy Island was expecting a particular guest. A guest that Uncle Sam has an interest in."

"Will that guest be checking in today?"

He eyed her. "Not anymore."

"Should I be expecting additional patients?"

He shook his head and straightened up. Slowly. His color wasn't ideal, but it had improved. "As soon as the weather clears, we'll get you off the island."

Figured. He left or she left. That was the story of her life.

"Am I in danger?" Risking her life would be stupid.

He exhaled harshly. "Not if you take orders and stay put."

"Fun times for me."

"As soon as the weather clears, we can get you off the island."

"Offer noted." But she wasn't sure she *wanted* to leave. "Keep the wound clean and dry. No swimming, no strenuous activity, so keep covert assaults to the minimum. After twenty-four hours, you can remove the bandage and wash the area with soap and water." She leveled him with a look. "Spread an antibiotic ointment over the site and reapply the bandage. I'm also putting you on a course of oral antibiotics."

"Yes, Doctor." This time his voice held a thread of amusement. The bastard was feeling better. "But that's a pass on the painkillers."

Of course. Because he was Superman and impervious to pain.

Knowing he was a rough-and-tough SEAL explained his dominant side, but it also meant she'd *never* been in charge of their relationship. He'd been in control from day one, both in bed and out. The smart part of her demanded an immediate evacuation of the island—her fiancé had certainly taught her the dangers of men who wouldn't open up and share—but another part of her wanted more. More Gray, more pleasure and a chance to explore the darker side of passion…

Sam rose to his feet, packing up his kit and disposing of the used gauze in a plastic bag. "Take it easy, okay? You don't have to save the world singlehandedly this morning. It can wait until tomorrow or next week."

Naturally, Gray didn't say anything. He was Mr. Stoic, keeping his feelings to himself. She got that he was no fan of opening up, but she needed words from him.

"Here's a hint," she said in a clipped voice. "We're having a conversation. I say something. You say something. It works like tennis or ping-pong."

"Or tossing a live hand grenade back and forth," Levi added helpfully.

Gray cursed. "There are things I can't talk about."

No kidding. "If you tell me this is one of those *things*, I might scream."

"Fair warning." He looked around the room at their audience. "Out."

Her nipples tightened at the command in his voice as everyone else jumped to obey. Staying professional with this man was impossible.

"I expected details," Ashley said, brushing past her and making for the door.

"Only if *I'm* still talking to you."

Ashley clearly had a double life, too, and Laney wasn't sure how she felt about that.

"Point taken." The other woman patted her on the arm. "But we're friends, so I'm holding out hope for a conversation later today."

Levi paused, hand on the door. "Sorry about the chokehold."

"No worries." She'd send him the therapy bills.

Levi, Mason and Gray had some kind of unspoken guy exchange among the three of them involving pointed looks and head nods. Whatever. Levi and Mason left, leaving her alone with Gray. *Finally.* She snapped off her gloves and tossed them in the trash.

"Is this the part where you tell me you have to kill me if I talk?"

He gave her The Look. Too bad. She wasn't backing down on this one. God. How could she have been so stupid? She might not have the best track record with men, but she knew Gray wouldn't hurt her. Of course, she was also rethinking what she knew about him. He was a soldier and a covert operative. He did things—secret, really important things—where people got hurt. Staying pissed off at him was petty. She could admit that to herself, because it was also personal. She'd always been good at imagining an intimate connection where there was none. Case in point: Harlan.

"No. This is the part where I say *thank you.*" He reached out and brushed the hair off her cheek. The desire rising up in her was both unexpected and irritating. He'd lied to her. She was unofficially his doctor. Either was a good reason to give him the cold shoulder, but her body apparently had other plans. Before she could give in to the urge to nuzzle the big hand cupping her cheek, she stepped away from him—not that she had much space to go far because the room was too damned small—and scrubbed her hands in the sink again.

Naturally, he followed her. "You're not into *thank-yous*?"

Tired of his games, she whirled and thrust a hand against his chest. "Back it up and answer one question for me. Was the sex just another lie?"

Terrific. Laney Parker was pissed as hell. It was kind of cute, although he was beyond certain that he'd lose his balls if he told her that. He also owed her big-time for sewing him up. Sam did his best, but a field medic was no match for a skilled trauma surgeon. So he was definitely telling her thank you, whether she liked it or not. And apparently, thanking her included answering her questions.

He braced his palm on the wall beside her head. Not because he was going for the sexy but because, damn it, he was feeling lightheaded and he needed the support. If he passed out and landed on her, he'd either squash her flat or make more work for her. "I should say *thank you* for the sex, too."

"Answer me." She poked him in the chest again. "Was Mr. Big, Bad Biker SEAL taking *undercover* to a whole new level?"

"The sex was not an act."

"Uncle Sam doesn't hire his boys out?"

Hell, no. He would have thought that was obvious, but the answer clearly mattered to her. "I wanted to have sex with you."

Wait. That didn't sound right.

She dug her finger into his chest again. He was going to have permanent divots there.

"You told me you worked here. You let me proposition you."

Definitely pissed off. But from the get-go, he'd made it clear he wasn't a nice guy. And, hell, she'd seemed to enjoy it, at least in bed. Unfortunately, when he leaned in a little more, he staggered and she busted him.

"Sit." She pointed to the bed. "Before you fall over and I have to patch something else up."

He sat. Guess he could take orders, after all.

"Is that what you do on all of your undercover missions? Hook up with the locals?"

"Do I need a lawyer?" he asked, his lips quirking.

"As in *anything you say can and will be used against you*?"

"A heads-up would be appreciated, yeah."

She sank onto the bed beside him. "Fair warning. I've been known to hold a grudge, and it's been one hell of a day."

He knew that feeling. He had a twin bed, a sink and his duffel bag underneath the bed. He needed a shower, a change of clothes and about forty-eight hours of shuteye because he was running on empty and his side hurt like a bitch. Still, he was shocked by the uncharacteristic need to pull her down on the bed with him, to wrap himself around her and just sleep.

"So. About our fantasy..."

Our. "Yeah? What about it?"

"Did you enjoy it?"

Oh, boy. What was it with this need she had to postmortem everything?

"Of course." That was the only right answer and they both knew it. That it happened to be true was a bonus. "You did, too."

His words weren't a question. He'd been there. He'd felt her coming, squeezing his dick as she called his name. So he could tell she'd enjoyed herself in the moment. Afterward, though, well, that might have been a different story. He knew all about sex and regrets. And he knew another thing, too. She didn't want to hear about the emptiness inside him, the way he used sex to fill that void. Bottom line? He was a guy attracted to a gorgeous woman with some really hot secret desires.

And because he'd not only bled all over her but lied to her about who he was and why he was on Fantasy Island, he'd be lucky if she shared any more of those desires with him. Although he wanted her to. *Badly.* Because Laney Parker was fast becoming his very own fantasy.

"I thought we were getting to know each other," she said in a hurt tone, then stood up, heading for the door. She didn't wait for his answer before stepping outside and closing the door behind her. But then it hadn't really been a question, had it? He wasn't the man she'd thought he was.

10

WHEN LANEY SLIPPED out of the room, blinking back angry tears, she found Ashley waiting in the hall. There was no visible sign of Mason, although she suspected he hadn't gone far. His absence was too bad—part of her still wanted to kick the man—hard—for letting her walk into Gray's room blind. Her back hurt from Levi's up-against-the-wall routine.

Ashley fell into step beside her. "I'll walk you back to your bungalow."

"Afraid I'll get lost?" She'd thought she and Ashley were on their way to becoming friends, but apparently, she'd misread the situation. Whoever this woman was, Laney was willing to bet she hadn't won her tickets to Fantasy Island in a radio contest.

The bigger question was, who was Gray to her? He'd said he was a lieutenant commander and a US Navy SEAL. He'd been injured—in the line of duty—and the other people in the room had to be his team members or people in the know.

"Are you a SEAL, too?"

Ashley made a face. "No girls allowed on the boys' team."

"Then I'm guessing you're some other branch of the military."

"Close." Ashley followed her when she started up the path. "I'm DEA."

Wow. Not what she was thinking. It was really none of her business who Ashley worked for, except that she had led her to believe that Ashley was just another resort guest. Or maybe she was being oversensitive.

"Does Madeline know?"

Ashley shook her head. "And I'd appreciate it if you kept it that way. The fewer people who know, the better."

Honestly, she didn't know anyone who would believe her. Even Madeline was going to demand proof.

"You set me up with Gray. Was that part of the cover story?"

She didn't enjoy feeling stupid. Or gullible. In fact, both of those unpleasant emotions ranked at the top of her feelings-to-avoid-at-all-costs list. Gray had been her rebound man, a fun treat for herself. Sure, she hadn't been looking for something permanent, but somehow she'd expected honesty. Maybe Gray was just really, really good at covert ops, because she'd believed him when he'd said he wanted her.

So, okay, she'd fallen just a little bit for him.

Ashley jammed her hands into her pockets. It was hard to imagine her as some kind of cutthroat DEA agent when Laney looked at the Daisy Dukes and pink flip-flops, but her fierce intelligence and ability to think on her feet? She had to respect that. She would have made a fantastic trauma surgeon.

"I'm going to be blunt, okay?"

Right. As if Ashley had ever been anything *but*. "You've been holding back on me?"

"Only about my job description." Ashley strode up the path, flip-flops snapping against her heels. "Here's the thing. I like you. I like Gray. He's uptight and closed off and his idea of a fun time seems to involve motorcycles, biker bars and any fight that ends with broken beer bottles, but he's a great guy. You were looking for a rebound guy for some no-holds-barred sex, and I thought the two of you would be good for each other."

Did hot sex really count as *good for each other*?

"Fantasy Island also has a reputation for vacation hookups. He didn't know about the drinks menu until I told him." Ashley held up a finger when Laney opened her mouth. "And I told him only when he asked me, because apparently *you* had brought it up."

She had. "I wouldn't have—"

Come on to him. Told him my secret fantasies.

"Had sex with him if you'd known he was a SEAL and not a resort employee? Are you sure?" Ashley patted her on the back.

No. She wasn't. "Are all of the resort employees military?"

"No." Ashley grinned at her. "And that's where you come in."

"I don't think it's recruiting day."

"Think of it as an opportunity," Ashley coaxed. "Or an invitation to indulge in your very own SEAL fantasy."

Laney shook her head. "You're incorrigible."

"If Gray keeps on seeing you, it would help with his cover story. Just in case our target already has eyes on the ground here."

"Are you telling me it's my patriotic duty to sleep with Gray? Because I'm not buying it, but nice try."

Ashley grinned and stopped outside Laney's bungalow. "New tactic. Any chance you have a soldier fantasy?"

She did, but just for one particular soldier. And didn't that suck?

SNORKELING BENEATH THE pier was apparently the equivalent of crashing the local fish bar—loads of fish just hanging around the wooden piers. Or maybe the fish were bored and also waiting for the rain to stop. Laney had no idea. Fantasy Island, however, was definitely not living up to its reputation as a sunny retreat. The two days since she'd patched Gray up had passed in a wet blur. Not that resort living was all bad. The five extra pounds on her butt and the permanent aversion to making her own bed were testament to that.

Rain stung her back and her legs, destroying much of the visibility when she moved out from underneath the pier. Still, she'd spotted an orange-and-white clown fish, so she could check finding Disney fish in the wild off the bucket list. She didn't particularly want to be snorkeling in a rainstorm, but there were limited land-based activities in the rain, plus, she was avoiding a certain undercover SEAL.

She hadn't seen much of him in the past two days. Once or twice, their paths had crossed, but he'd nodded and kept right on walking. She hadn't even merited a conversation. Which was typical. Have sex, patch a guy up and the fantasy disintegrated. Boom. A slap in the face from reality right there on the spot. Today she'd avoided the massage cabanas as if the huts were an Ebola hotspot. Her new game was walking around the resort, trying to identify undercover SEALs. She'd ruled out the female guests—other than Ashley, who was more an honorary SEAL, anyhow, as far as Laney could tell—but the constant rain wasn't helping.

It was perfect sex weather.

Maybe that was her real problem. She drifted over to check out a particularly colorful clump of coral and considered the possibility. She'd had sex with Gray and it had been fantastic. It had also made her cranky. And horny. And, okay, more than a little bit depressed that what had been the hottest sex of her life apparently didn't rate so much as a repeat in *his* orbit. Of course, he was also busy leading a double life and a SEAL team, so possibly he didn't have time for vacation sex since he wasn't even on a vacation. Or maybe he was actually taking it easy and babying his gunshot wound and had temporarily crossed hot monkey sex off his to-do list.

Right. Just the thought made her snort, and *that* had her sucking in a mouthful of seawater. Popping upright, she treaded water while she emptied out the snorkel and her lungs. When she stuck her face back in the water, movement flashed in her peripheral vision. *Whoa. Big fish alert.* She turned and came face-to-face with a long, gray tube of a fish sporting a mouthful of teeth that would make a vampire proud. No blood-sucking for her, thank you very much. When it swam straight toward her, she bolted. Heart in her throat, she pretty much flew up the ladder, teetering in her fins when she neared the top. Except she didn't fall back. A sun-bronzed hand with a familiar dive watch wrapped around her wrist and lifted her up the last few rungs.

Well…shoot.

Mr. Fantasy in the flesh.

He steadied her effortlessly, as if he hadn't just hauled her not-so-featherweight self up the ladder one-handed. While she stared at him and wondered when he'd become her own personal elevator, he gave her a small smile and let go of her wrist. The powerful lines of his big, hard body were all too evident thanks to the rain and the white linen spa uniform he still wore. She had no idea how she'd ever bought the masseuse line, because he moved like a street fighter, all raw power and leashed menace. Yep. It was official. She could think of a few more fantasies to reenact with him.

He looked hot. She, on the other hand, looked like a first-class dork. She'd accessorized her practical black two-piece suit with a snorkel, mask and an inflatable snorkel vest because, okay, she panicked when the water got over her head and it wasn't safe to snorkel alone. Risking drowning to fish-spot was stupid. So was sporting the bright pink snorkel vest. Monster fish had probably taken one look at her bobbing along and decided he'd found himself a floating Twinkie. Gray didn't seem to mind, though. He held an oversize towel over their heads as if it was their own personal canopy.

"Fish biting today?" She liked the smile in his eyes as he spoke, even if she had no idea why he was out here. Maybe it was part of the secret SEAL mission to recon the pier for enemy soldiers and errant snorkelers. Lucky her.

"You have no idea." She pulled off the mask and started squeezing air out of the vest. "There's something down there with more teeth than a piranha and it's way too friendly."

Or unfriendly.

He transferred the towel to her and dropped down onto his haunches, gently tugging on her ankle. Off balance, she rested a hand on his shoulder and lifted obediently so he could slide the first fin off.

He looked up at her, a slow grin tugging at his mouth. "Long fish with dark scales and a little shark-fin thing at the back?"

He moved his hands apart to indicate size. *Close.*

"Keep going. Fantasy Island stocks monster fish."

He nodded and pulled the second fin off. "Barracuda. He'll chase you off. Be a little aggressive because you're swimming in his territory. Next time you see Mason, ask him about the barracuda that chased him in the Indian Ocean. He never saw it coming until it tried to take a chunk out of his ass. He caught it and barbecued it."

Typical. "That fish must be a male."

"Do I want to know?" Gray stood up and grabbed her fins. Was that the equivalent of carrying her books home from school? Damn it. She needed an instruction manual or a dating guide. Something.

Since he'd asked for it, she should tell him. She'd be doing the future women in his life a favor. "He got himself a piece of ass and ran." She shrugged when Gray stared at her. "What? That fits your story and mine."

"Don't be difficult." He started walking down the dock, oblivious to the rain. Since she wasn't about to let him have the last word, she followed him. Plus, he had her fins and she had to return them to the water sports hut.

"I can be difficult if I want," she muttered and he shook his head. Maybe it was time for a change of subject. She eyed his wet T-shirt, but couldn't tell if he was still in pain.

"How's the side?"

"Fine." He shrugged, but she was a trained professional. She'd dealt with more than her fair share of grown men pretending their injuries were mere scratches.

"Let me see."

He gave her a look. The one that said *even if I'm impaled by half the dock, I'm not admitting to any discomfort.* Men! "On a scale of one to ten, it's not even a whole number."

"I'm still looking. Welcome to the tropics. A little bacteria, a little sepsis…and *boom*, you're dead."

Losing Gray would be a waste.

"Cheerful." He shook his head. "And things go *boom* all the time in my line of work."

"My room. Your room. A third party, neutral space. Pick a spot, because I'm looking at your side."

"Bossy."

"Doctor," she countered. Never mind that she was soaked to the skin, in a bikini and barefoot. Her outfit wasn't exactly white coat material, but he didn't seem to mind. *There.* The towel hut was a little cabana thing with a thatched roof and a wide-open door. It appeared to be mostly shelves of white towels, but there was also a decent overhead light. She could make do and it would be far less depressing than dragging him back to her bungalow and having nothing happen besides a medical checkup. "Pit stop."

To her surprise, he let her steer him into the towel hut. Of course, he didn't seem in any hurry to get naked, which just brought her back to her original problem. They'd done it and now *he* was done. She swallowed her disappointment, reminding herself that right now it didn't matter. Even if he didn't want a lover, he still got the doctor.

She pointed to his T-shirt. Despite his best attempts to shield them with the towel, Gray was soaked, which was not ideal. Bullet wounds liked to stay dry. "Off."

With a sigh, he stripped off his shirt. Mother Nature liked him, too. Water drops trickled down his taut abdomen and just begged her to lick him clean. Or dirty. She really wasn't picky when it came to Gray.

"I'm fine," he said. "Sam's been checking me out."

"I went to med school for approximately a thousand years to do this. I'm better." Carefully, she peeled back the dressing. There were no signs of infection, and he actually hadn't ripped out his stitches. Which was probably a miracle, because she doubted Mr. SEAL had really been taking it easy.

"You're also mad at me," he pointed out drolly. "I'm not sure that guarantees a sympathetic bedside manner."

"Two words. *Hippocratic Oath*."

"Good to know."

His side looked good. Since he was undoubtedly doing macho manly SEAL things, rather than engaging in bed rest, that was a small miracle. And damn it, she had to stop thinking of beds and Gray at the same time.

"Is Mason really a cook?" she asked, to take her mind off sex.

Gray grinned. "He's cooking. Does that count?"

She thought about that for a minute.

"The rain means no seaplanes are flying," he continued, his smile fading. "The visibility is too low. I'd prefer to get you off the island. Get you somewhere safe."

Gray obviously hadn't gotten the memo on Ashley's

cover story plan. "My reservation has a few nights left to go. I'm not planning on sleeping on the beach."

She was tired of throwing in the towel and running. She'd run when Harlan's affair had come to light, and she didn't like herself for that. Gray might be a SEAL and he might be here on an undercover op, but she had a right to be here, too. Plus, she found his insistence on keeping her safe sweet. Which was ridiculous. She was grasping at straws. He was a decent guy and a SEAL. Protecting her came with the territory. He could hardly insist on putting her *in* danger.

"Do I pass inspection?" he asked, dropping the subject of her departure. She had a feeling the subject wasn't closed, however.

"Um. Yeah." She pressed the bandage back in place.

"Good." He pulled her upright and swung her around. "Because I want a shot. Any objections?"

He braced her against the wall, flattening his palm beside her head as his inner caveman came out to play. Unfortunately, her inner cavewoman was in full agreement.

"At…?" She really needed clarification here.

"A second night. A second fantasy."

"I'm your doctor."

"Temporarily and by accident," he pointed out.

"Sex between us isn't appropriate. It's also a really, really bad idea."

"You don't want to do your patriotic duty?" Hell. The line sounded cheesy, even to *him*, and Gray had never won awards for his smooth-talking charm. That was Levi's area of expertise. Blow shit up. Charm the panties off the ladies. Levi was a pro.

"You're under doctor's orders." She eyed him glee-fully. "You have to do what I say."

Military doctors on two continents hadn't been able to compel him to follow orders. He grinned up at her. He liked looking at Laney, even when he was actually staring at the top of her head while her cool hands examined the gunshot wound in his side. He'd been lucky. The bullet had taken a shortcut across his side, but it hadn't gone through. He'd be fine. Hell, he'd had worse.

"Come by tonight and I'll change the bandage." Her head was close enough to his bare skin that he felt her words against it, the tiny puff of air as she exhaled. Knowing Laney, she was likely irritated or pissed off.

"Laney." Her name was a start. Unfortunately, he had absolutely no idea what to say next.

"Ashley said I could help you with your cover story," she said, veering off on a tangent.

"She did?" He needed to kill Ashley. Slowly. He appreciated her concern for his sex life—*not*—but she had to stop meddling. Maybe she was bored or liked the fire-works. He had no idea, but being near Laney was torturing him, and he didn't need any more encouragement.

"She said that it was possible your target had eyes on the ground and that you all needed to stay in character until you complete your mission." She shrugged. She was close enough that the move had her breasts brushing against his chest. Her thin bikini top was nowhere near enough fabric. Her nipples were hard little points raking his chest. Was she cold—or aroused? Did she want to pick up where they'd left off the other night? Because his dirty fantasy count definitely exceeded one. When he didn't say anything, Laney rushed to fill in the awkward silence.

"*She* said Fantasy Island has a certain reputation."

He needed to tread carefully. Laney's claim was more explosive than an ambush with claymores. "It's an exotic island getaway. It's supposed to be fun."

Laney elbowed him. Hard. Gray was almost certain she deliberately went for his good side. "For the drinks menu," she said. "People come here, they share their fantasies and…"

Boom.

Her blush was cute. Her face resembled a sunburned tomato, which he found amusing. She'd do it, but she wouldn't say it? They'd have to work on her vocabulary.

"We shared a fantasy." Pointing out the truth was the honest thing to do.

"I know." She glared at him. "*One* fantasy."

"Is the problem with the quantity or the quality?" Her hair was drying into little wayward ringlets. She had a cowlick, too, the piece sticking straight out at an impossible angle. His fingers itched to reach out and smooth the wayward strands into place. Laney was mussed up, and *he* definitely had an issue with the quantity of his fantasies because he had plural fantasies. As in, more than one and more than once. He didn't do long-term. Hell, he rarely went back for seconds, and he'd be the first to admit that made him a dick.

"Ashley thinks we should keep pretending to have a relationship."

Huh. Ashley actually had a point.

"Ashley wants us to pretend to have sex."

"I don't think *pretend* was what she had in mind. Ashley's open-minded."

And then some. Ashley had a one-night rule herself. Levi had bitched about it more than once.

"I'm not pretending to have sex with you."

"Wow," she said. "Thanks for the confidence booster."

Was that hurt in her eyes? Because he wasn't *that* much of a dick. Not intentionally. "I definitely want to have sex with you. Real sex," he added softly, when she didn't say anything. This was why one-nighters were simpler. More sex, less talking.

She pursed her lips. "Ashley made this sound easy."

There wasn't a single easy thing about them. He knew that. And so did she.

"It would bolster my cover story," he said helpfully. Honestly, he had no idea if Marcos had spies on Fantasy Island. If he did, it seemed even more far-fetched that said spies would be less inclined to spot Gray for what and who he was if he was having sex with one of the resort guests. However, he was still selfish. And he wanted Laney Parker. So…he'd run with it. "If you pretended to be my vacation hookup."

She nodded. "Pretend relationship. Real sex. I can work with that, but just for the record, I still think having sex with you is a bad idea."

"But?"

"But I'm going to do it, anyhow." She sighed.

"Tonight. My place." He forced himself to step away from her, before he did something really stupid, like gather her up in his arms in the towel hut. Her soft protest followed him as he left.

"Wait. We should set a time."

He wasn't scheduling sex with her. He wanted to be more than another to-do in her phone. "When you want me, come and find me," he said and slipped out into the rain.

11

LANEY STEPPED ONTO the path leading to the resort's employee housing. This was crazy. She should turn around and go back to her bungalow. But anticipation fizzed through her, and she knew she wasn't going anywhere but forward. To Gray. The sun had set and the lights lining the path had come on. Since he had refused to pick a time for their date—and she'd decided to call it a *date* rather than *casual vacation sex hookup*—she'd waited until night fell. Fantasy sex and darkness seemed to go together.

In addition to being unsure of the time, she wasn't sure of the dress code for an early-evening sex date. In the end, she'd gone with a red-and white-striped sundress. The dress tied around her neck with two delicate strings that ended in tiny brass beads and brushed against the bare skin of her back. It made her feel sexy, and sexy was good. Heels weren't happening with the resort's gravel path, plus, she clumped ungracefully in anything other than flats, so she'd settled on a pair of cute sandals. And she'd gone all out and added lip gloss. Woo-hoo. Her feminine arsenal definitely needed restocking. As a newbie surgeon working eighty-hour weeks, she hadn't had time for date clothes.

Not that Gray seemed to mind.

He seemed to like her just the way she was. Although he definitely had a preference for naked.

She liked him naked, too.

Someone stepped out onto the path behind her. She didn't hear him move. One second, she was alone and the next, a big, hard body pressed up against hers. Maybe they included ninja classes at BUD/S training. Even as she recognized him, her heartbeat picked up in anticipation. Her imagination immediately kicked in, too, suggesting all sorts of naughty possibilities.

"If you give me a heart attack, neither of us is going to enjoy tonight," she said lightly as Gray set his hands on her hips and tugged her back against him. Where else would he put his hands? He wasn't an *ask first, act second* man and, as un-PC as it was, she loved that about him.

"Tonight's my turn," he growled.

Ooh. He was as good at being cryptic as he was at super stealth.

"And hello to you, too." She wriggled backward and, yep, he was definitely glad to see her even if his verbal greeting left something to be desired. She could feel his mighty impressive erection through his pants, and that part of him was definitely perfect. She also liked the way he held on to her. Okay, she liked it a lot. She wasn't going anywhere until he said so, and the feeling of powerlessness was an unexpected turn-on.

"Your place?" She prompted, when he didn't move. She definitely wasn't doing it on the path. Not only were they in a very public spot, but there would also be insects. Crickets or mutant jungle bugs whined from the dense screen of palm trees nearby. No way she was exposing flesh around *them*.

He leaned down, his mouth brushing her ear. "Last chance to back out."

Hello. "I came out here for a reason. I'm not leaving now."

He nipped her ear. The tiny bite stung, followed by a wave of molten pleasure that should have embarrassed her. Apparently, however, she was shameless tonight because she let out a small moan, and his lips curved upward in a smile.

Pressed up against him, she could feel the hard muscles of his thighs and chest. The man didn't have a soft inch anywhere. Her position was both hot—and awkward. Her butt was glued against his front, and she wasn't entirely sure where to put her hands. She settled for placing them on his forearms. He was all corded muscle there, too. She'd be a lucky woman if she could get him inside and get his clothes off. And if his heart didn't have a soft spot for her, she was okay with that. Assuming his words were man code for *don't expect anything but sex from me.* That fit her plans just fine, right? The way his erection pressed into her butt, his good parts rubbing against hers, also fit in just fine. Except…she'd have taken more if he'd been offering. More sex, more caring, more *Gray.* Darn it. He'd worked his way inside her heart like a SEAL on a convert op and she'd never seen him coming.

Evidently, he wasn't done with his public service announcement, however, because he kept on talking. "Unless you walk away right now, I'll make you open up in every way possible. I'll take charge, own every inch of your gorgeous body, inside and out."

Wow. "That sounds like a plan."

Count her in. She tugged forward, and this time he let her move. The short walk to his room was strangely companionable. He threaded his fingers through hers, and she wanted to point out that he was holding her hand, which probably broke one of their hard-and-fast rules, but there was no sense in poking the bear, at least not until after she'd got what she came for. Plus, she could practically feel him gearing up to talk.

"If you ask me if I'm sure again, I'm going to hit you," she warned.

A husky laugh escaped him, and she wondered which of them was more surprised. He needed to laugh more, to take life a little less seriously. It wasn't all war games and death missions. He might be able to teach her about kinky sex, but maybe she could teach him something, too. That with the right person, at the right time, sex was fun. And she planned on having plenty of fun tonight.

"I want to be here," she admitted softly. "With you."

"Why?" He sounded genuinely curious as he unlocked the door to his room and gestured for her to go in first.

"No booby traps?"

He gave her a look. "That's why I'm sending you in first."

She grinned. "Glad I didn't pick you because you were a gentleman."

HE ABSOLUTELY WANTED to believe that she'd picked him. The reasons didn't matter so much, although he couldn't be a gentleman if his life depended on it. Laney Parker drove him crazy. From her methodical, let's-schedule-

everything-including-sex approach to life to the way
she stared at him as if he was the most mouthwatering
brownie on the plate and she planned on having him.
Now. Maybe he drove her a little bit crazy, too.

As he followed her inside his room, he realized something else. Laney dressed up for date night drove him
more than a little crazy. His awareness of her was a ten
on the Richter scale, her sassy sundress begging to be
stripped off as she strolled into his room with a sexy roll
of her hips. Giving in to temptation, he ran his fingers
down the exposed line of her spine. Her dress dipped almost to her waist in the back, a clear hint that she wore
no bra. The only thing between him and all her pretty,
sun-kissed skin was a handful of cotton.

He pulled her back against him and wrapped one arm
around her waist. With his other hand, he tilted her chin
up and kissed her. A hard, demanding kiss because if
she wasn't ready for this, for him, he needed to know.
For her, he'd slow things down, kiss her until he got it
right. He bit her lower lip, catching the plump flesh between his teeth. She tasted like raspberries, pink and
tart where she'd slicked some sort of gloss over her lips.
He licked her once, twice, then swept inside her mouth
when she gasped.

But she pressed back against him, her tongue flirting with his, and when he increased the pressure of his
mouth, she moaned. She moved her hands, too, stroking his arms, petting his thighs, as if she couldn't get
enough of him. And then she drew back.

"Wait," she said.

Crap. He'd scared her. "Laney—"

She wriggled around, turning in his hold until she

faced him. "So much better," she sighed, tipping her head back. "Carry on."

She was right.

He backed her toward the bed, suddenly grateful for the room's small size. Five steps and her knees hit the mattress. The room's lack of romantic extravagance was a plus. Hell, the place was downright sterile. As a resort "employee," he merited four walls, one door, one window. He also had a twin bed, a set of plain white sheets and a navy blue comforter, none of which he'd put to much use because he'd spent most of his downtime in the SEAL camp. Frankly, the difference between this room and Laney's bungalow was the difference between, say, Siberia and Fiji. It probably mirrored the differences between the two of them, as well.

"Can we have sex now? Please?" She tugged at his T-shirt.

"I want you to try something for me first."

"What?"

Reaching into his pocket, he pulled out a pair of silk ties. Usually, he would have used whatever was handy— a cord, a length of rope, his belt. But for her, he'd wanted something special and one of a kind, because she was all he could think about. Thank God none of his team had spotted him going into the hotel gift shop where he'd picked out a pair of pink silk ties while the saleslady smirked at him from behind the counter. But it had been worth the small amount of humiliation on his part. The fabric was soft and wouldn't burn her skin. He'd also be able to free her easily if she panicked.

"I want to tie you up."

She made a sound, her face flushing. But she didn't take her gaze off the ties in his hand. Then she looked up at him, her eyes glazed with a sweet, lush need. "What do I do?"

He set the ties down on the bed and then reached for the strings around her neck holding her dress together. One good tug and they parted, just like he'd imagined. The cotton slipped to her waist when she wiggled. She liked what she was doing, or maybe she just liked turning him on, because her nipples were tight, her breasts flushed.

"Look at these waiting for me." He cupped her breasts, rubbing his thumbs over the hard tips.

The dress hit the floor.

Laney hooked her thumbs in the waistband of her panties. She must have toed off her sandals because that scrap of black lace was all she wore. And, Jesus, she wore it well. The wicked black vee barely skimmed her mound. She was all shadowy curves and sweet, decadent temptation in the dark room.

"Leave the panties. Kneel on the bed and put your hands on the headboard."

She hesitated. "I love these panties."

So did he.

She eyed him sternly. "So no ripping or tearing. My credit card is still protesting the price tag."

He grinned. He'd buy her a dozen in every color of the rainbow. When she climbed up on the bed, heat exploded through him at her unwavering trust. His skin felt too tight, his balls aching and his dick hard enough to hammer iron.

Reaching over her, he bound her left wrist to the bedpost.

"No bow?" She sounded breathless, but he could hear the laughter in her voice. She wasn't nervous or scared.

She was excited and curious. God, he loved her curiosity. Almost as much as he loved her trust. His brain skirted dangerous territory for a minute. *Love* wasn't part of his vocabulary.

Was it?

"Beautiful." He pressed a kiss against her bare shoulder as he tied her right wrist to the bedpost. "I wish you could see yourself."

"No photos," she said, turning her head to watch him as he stepped back from the bed. "Let me be really clear, in case that's where you were going with that."

His head took a right turn down fantasy lane, imagining the photos he could take of her. She'd be luscious, all her secrets on display for him, and he could take her out and look at her when they had an ocean between them once again. He'd have to convince her to give it a shot.

"I wouldn't share the photos," he said, his voice sounding hoarse, even to his own ears. "They'd be mine."

"Uh-huh. Now that you have me where you want me, what are you going to do with me?"

"Sweetheart, you're going to have to wait and see."

Her eyes narrowed as she shifted on the bed. "Seeing is fine. It's the waiting part I didn't sign up for."

"This is my night. I get to give the orders. Plus, you're not in any position to protest, are you?"

She tugged on her wrists, but he'd learned to tie knots with the US Navy. She wasn't going anywhere without his say-so.

"I enjoy looking at you," he added huskily. "So I plan to take my sweet time."

Touching her was his priority, though, so he stripped off his clothes swiftly. He wasn't strip-show material, but she watched him with hungry eyes and damned if he didn't feel like the king of the world. He undid her hair from its ponytail, sifting the silky strands around her bare shoulders.

Fucking gorgeous.

That was what she was.

OH, GOD. SHE'D never been so intensely aware of her body. Or her nakedness. Her knees pressed into his pillow, her fingers curled around the bedposts. Instead of feeling silly or wondering if she was doing this okay, however, she felt powerful. She could hear the harsh rasp of his breathing behind her. Seeing her like this turned him on. It turned her on, too.

He'd shocked her.

Aroused her.

And now he was actually *doing* it. Holy hell.

"I'm not into kinky stuff. No spanking," she added quickly, because *hello, pot*. She clearly liked some kinky stuff just fine. Pain, however, wasn't on her to-do list for tonight. Tonight she was all about the pleasure.

"Duly noted."

He ran his hand down her spine and over her butt, as if he was thinking about what to do next. She shivered in anticipation. She had a few thoughts of her own. "You could get naked, too, just to even things up."

"Shhh." He tapped the inside of her thigh. "Wider."

She didn't hesitate. She trusted him. She loved how he made her feel, how she could be open with him in a way she'd never been before. And she hadn't known that taking orders while tied up would make her feel so…powerful. Carefully, she slid her legs farther apart, drinking in the rough sound of pleasure he made.

He slid beneath her in a move too complex for her to

figure out, possibly because her brain had short-circuited sometime between his tethering her to his bed and his getting naked. She blamed any lack of thinking on him. She only had a moment to appreciate the eroticism of his position, because he was shoving her panties to one side.

"No tearing," he promised gruffly, and all she could do was moan. Because really? Her preserve-my-panties stance wasn't her top priority anymore. He exhaled and she felt *that*, too, and jerked, but the ties binding her to the bed held her in place.

And then she really stopped thinking. He swiped his tongue from the bottom of her slit to the top in one hot, luscious stroke.

"Hold on," he ordered and she did, fingers grabbing onto the headboard. There was nothing dignified about this, but she didn't have a choice, did she? All she could do was *feel*.

And boy, did he make her feel.

He spread her wider, licking and tonguing her slick folds. His tongue traced a wicked path, traveling up then back down again. Over and over as if he had all the time in the world, while she chanted a silent *more, more, more* and *oh, yes, please*. God, he was good. Or bad. She lost herself in the sweet bliss, letting him push her relentlessly toward the orgasm of the century.

When he found her clit, he wrung a new cry from her. She had no control, and he had it all, but she didn't feel powerless, didn't enjoy what he was doing to her any less because he was doing it *for* her.

"Gray—" She gasped his name, but she had no idea what came next. He did, though. He kissed her again and she trembled, reaching, trying to fall over the edge and succumb to the pleasure.

"Relax," he said. "I've got you."

He braced her thighs with his hands, anchoring her. With him, she wouldn't fall. It was hard to let go, harder not to. He licked and kissed, suckled her clit, and she surrendered. Sensation took over and she rocked against him, searching for more because she wanted everything this man would give her. And then she spasmed, her whole body clenching and holding on to him as she fell over the edge into that dark abyss of pleasure.

When she finally remembered where she was and her heart stopped pounding in her ears, he'd moved behind her.

"We're not done yet," he said, spreading her trembling thighs wider, and she closed her eyes in anticipation. The wet ache started up again, her body responding easily to his commands as he angled her forward, easing between her legs and parting her with his fingers.

He notched himself at her opening and pushed in. And then in some more. She inhaled sharply at the fullness. Still sensitive from the orgasm he'd just given her, she felt each thick, fantastic inch filling up her body.

"Slow or hard?" he gritted out, and all she could think was *now* and *more*.

"Hard." He'd already tortured her enough.

"You got it." He drove into her, stopping only when he was buried deep inside her, the tip of his cock bumping against her cervix. Then he pulled back, coming out of her only to drive inward again, finding a rhythm that drove her crazy. She waited for each thrust, soaring higher and higher with each new stroke. Heat filled her as she surrendered to the crazy-hard rhythm of sex, the bed squeaking and groaning as he slammed into her, and she arched back to take him harder, deeper, *more*.

"Now." He reached between them, pinching her clit.

"Wait." She didn't want to lose this sensation, the near-mindless bliss as they took each other.

"Yes," he hissed. He drove into her again, nipping at the curve of her throat and she lost it, coming again, clenching around him and holding him tight. Like her pleasure was the permission slip he'd needed, he hammered into her hard, coming with her as he whispered her name over and over as if it was his passport to someplace special he couldn't wait to be.

12

HE DIDN'T WANT to untie her. He did it, anyway, because Laney trusted him and leaving her bound to the bed, while fun for him, would probably scare the crap out of her until she figured out the hitch knots came undone easily. The pretty pink ties were silky smooth, the material running through his fingers like water. And that was part of the game, wasn't it? She could slip away from him just as easily.

"You okay?" He rubbed a thumb over her wrists. The ties had left faint marks. He pressed his lips against her pinkened skin. The gesture wasn't smooth, and he was definitely tipping his hand, but he did it, anyhow. As strong as she was, the bones of her wrist felt delicate, pale blue veins visible beneath the skin.

"I thought you weren't a fan of the post-mortem," she murmured sleepily. He'd worn her out, or maybe that was the multiple orgasms. Leaping on top of the covers and beating his chest seemed too caveman-like, so he settled for tucking the ties away in the pants he swiped from the floor. *Souvenir.* Something to remember her by when she'd left the island and he'd completed his mission here. She'd go home—and he'd go find himself a new battlefield.

"You were beautiful," he whispered roughly.

"That was one hell of a fantasy, and you're amazing." She shifted, burrowing in and getting comfortable. He was losing her to the bed. "When can we do it again?"

His dick voted for now as she settled her butt against his front and inched closer. But she hadn't been talking about the sex being *amazing*. At least he didn't think so. She'd said *he* was amazing. It made him feel good, better than good, but it also meant it was time to retreat. Things were getting too personal between them. Making Laney's sexual fantasies come true was great, but he couldn't give her anything else. He was all body, no heart. And she deserved more. He didn't know how to love someone—let alone say *I love you* or commit to any future more than a week out. All of which meant he needed to pull back, put some space between them and act like a Boy Scout—hands off.

His libido—and possibly a different organ higher up—protested.

"Gray?" Her sleepy voice was half-muffled by the pillow she'd buried her face in.

"Yeah?" He reached over to switch off the light. He'd like to make love to her in the daylight, watch her face as she came. Then he could watch all the little expressions on her face, see the pucker she got on her forehead as she concentrated on his touch and the way she bit her lower lip. They hadn't done daylight sex. Somehow fantasies seemed like midnight material. "I'm right here."

"Hold me?" She didn't wait for his agreement. Instead, she rolled over and flopped onto his chest, her fingers tangling in his dog tags as she planted her head over his heart.

Did he know how to get the holding thing right? Because she wasn't just asking him to put his arm around her, was she? It was part of that whole *Gray, you're amazing* problem. She was asking him to cozy up emotionally and for that she needed a different man.

Over my dead body, his traitorous heart protested.

"Don't overthink it." She grinned up at him sleepily. "Holding me isn't rocket science."

No, but getting it right mattered. Making her *happy* mattered. He was screwed here in ways far beyond the sexual. He tucked an arm around her and settled back against the mountain of pillows she'd accumulated from somewhere. One bed. One pillow. That was how his bed had always worked, because he didn't do sleepovers. Instead, she had enough pillows for two SEAL units.

"Scoot down some," she mumbled. "We need to work on your cuddling skills."

As he processed that, she proceeded to bang her head around his rib cage, her chin digging into his chest, as she made herself comfortable. Eventually, she settled for draping one leg over his, her arm tucked around his middle. He had no idea where she'd managed to store the other arm, but it seemed like an anatomical impossibility.

"See? Isn't that better?" Her hair tickled his armpit, and if she moved too quickly, he'd be singing soprano. So okay. It was also pretty damn perfect. He could do this. He should probably tell her how amazing she'd been or how gorgeous she looked. She'd complimented him, after all, so he needed to level the playing field some.

"Thank you," he said, instead. Because it turned out that was what he meant.

He felt her smile against his skin. "You're one hell of a rebound guy."

Ouch. So maybe he wasn't so amazing, after all. Maybe he was just fantasy fodder, the guy who could bring her dreams to life *temporarily*. Feeling hurt was stupid. He should let it go.

"Who was he?" Nope. Apparently, he was holding on with both hands.

"Who was who?" Her drowsy mumble wasn't encouraging. Laney was clearly no night owl. He had no idea how she'd made it through med school—likely on sheer determination. That fit the Laney he was coming to know.

"The first guy."

He waited for her to say something. Her fingers played with his dog tags, brushing against his skin. The pale band of skin he'd noticed on her ring finger during their first massage was getting steadily harder to see as the Caribbean sun turned her skin a rich golden brown.

"Harlan was my fiancé," she said finally.

"Past tense?" Had to be, though. She wasn't the kind of woman to cheat, and she'd come to Fantasy Island minus a ring.

"This was supposed to be our honeymoon." Her voice sounded wistful. "He cheated on me. I caught him with a nurse, having sex on a gurney. Guess he had fantasies of his own."

White-hot fury lashed through him. He could make a few calls, round up a SEAL unit to go after Harlan. Instead, he tightened his arm carefully around her. "He's an idiot."

"I know that. *Now.*" Amusement colored her voice.

"And truly, it was better to find out before we got married. It's just—"

He wasn't good at this talking thing. He was probably supposed to make sympathetic noises or curse the guy out. Instead, he petted her hair, smoothing his hand over strands that were even silkier than the ties he'd used to bind her in place. Little pieces stuck up, tickling his nose when he leaned down.

"But what?" He made a sound, low and rough, but it wasn't right, either. He sounded as if he had a mutant-sized frog in his throat. She didn't seem to mind, though, because she kept right on talking.

"But apparently, I wasn't *his* fantasy. I just wasn't… enough. Or right. He didn't even give me the chance. I thought we were friends and partners, as well as lovers. And I had that wrong, too."

"You're right for me." He waited for the urge to leave to hit him, but it was AWOL. Still, he didn't have a damn clue what he was doing here. Pleasing her body, bringing her to orgasm—those were things he was good at. He also knew how to write a rent check and pay the electric, but otherwise he was a relationship virgin. If she wanted anything more from him, she'd got the wrong man.

GRAY'S HEART BEAT out a rock-steady rhythm beneath her cheek. She figured he'd face down any number of crises with the same calm. For a moment she let her imagination place him in various ridiculous scenarios. Stampeding elephants, a zombie invasion, the Colombian Navy storming the beach on Fantasy Island…

It was easier than imagining this thing they had going anywhere further than bed. She had no complaints about their chemistry. The sex had been amazing and erotic and also scary as hell because he hadn't let her hold anything back. She'd been open to him in every way possible and open meant vulnerable. And that vulnerability definitely meant she should stop asking him questions. Eventually, she'd get an answer she didn't like because he clearly wasn't into sharing how he felt. Possibly because he didn't feel anything remotely Hallmark-like for her. They'd had hot vacation sex, and she shouldn't overthink things.

And yet...

Yeah. She was doing a lot of thinking.

She wanted to get to know *him*. Not just his body or what got him off. She already recognized the way his breathing got harsher and faster when he was close to coming, the way he fisted the sheets and the hungry edge to the way he touched her. He drove her crazy, turned her on and gave her the best sex of her life. She'd be an idiot to complain about that.

On the other hand, she was feeling emotionally bare and she *hated* that. She shifted his dog tags through her fingers, turning the metal so she could read it in the dim light. JACKSON GRAY R. A blank line and then his social security number and blood type. NORELPREF. Somehow, the lack of information didn't surprise her.

"What's the *R* for?"

He tugged lightly on her hair. "Would you believe Radcliff?"

"It doesn't sound as if I should."

"Rafe? Remus? Rochester?"

"Be serious. Is your middle name really a national secret?"

He shrugged. "Randall. After my dad."

"Was he a SEAL, too?"

"He didn't stick around after I was born. It was just my mom and me."

"That sounds like it might have sucked."

"Only sometimes," he said softly. "I was a trailer park kid in a farming community. My mom worked her ass off to put food on the table and keep the electric on. We might have had canned peaches instead of fresh, but she did the best she could even if sometimes the canned stuff came from the church pantry and not the grocery store."

"She sounds special."

"Uh-huh. I gave her plenty of hell. Fighting came easier than words, and between the kids at school and my cousins, I was always fighting."

The words came sliding out before she could bite them back. "So how did you become a SEAL?"

"My cousins and I, we ran as a pack, got into trouble as a pack. We rode bikes from an early age, made the highway our racetrack. My oldest cousin got himself in trouble with a neighbor's daughter. I never did find out exactly what he'd done, but her dad and his decided it was my cousin's golden opportunity to enlist in the US Navy. It was the only get-out-of-jail-free card they'd give him, and he took it. And where he went, I went."

"To BUD/S and the SEALs."

He grinned. "I may have taken it a little further than my cousin."

"It's your turn." She stared up at him expectantly. "Pick a drink. Share your fantasy with me."

Not in a million years. He shouldn't have come here, but apparently, *self-control* and *restraint* were words that didn't apply when he was around Laney. Unless the *restraint* in question was a pair of fur-lined handcuffs. Who knew the gift shop stocked novelty items like that?

He'd grown up on the wrong side of the tracks—hell, he'd driven his bike down the track at eighty miles an hour and played chicken with the oncoming train. Laney had no idea what she was unleashing if she dared him to name his fantasies. Still, her naughty grin was contagious. If she wanted to play, he was game. *"A Short Southern Screw?"*

"Ugh." She made a face. "What makes sex Southern versus Northern? Or Eastern or Western?"

Good question, but one he couldn't answer. Next suggestion. *"Ball and Chain?"*

"Sounds like a bad wedding joke." Her smile died, and tracking down her ex-fiancé moved to the top of his to-do list.

"Bikini Line? Cowboy Up? Geisha?"

"You're into costumes and having sex incognito? Oh. Right. Covert SEAL op. Check, check and check."

He'd had her already tonight and it seemed as if she was offering seconds. Except that wasn't how he really thought of her. She wasn't a count or a notch on his belt, or even a hot woman who'd come on to him. She was just Laney.

His Laney.

And that scared him more than a little. So, yeah, he had fantasies. He'd fantasized about taking her a dozen different ways, each kinkier than the last. Tying her up, spreading her open, licking and sucking and tonguing her until she came. Then he'd do it all over again. Maybe the drink he should be ordering was the *Green-Eyed Monster*, because when he thought about her douchebag ex, he wanted to rip the man apart. Mostly because he'd hurt Laney, but also because Gray was jealous. The *J* word.

He was never jealous, any more than he was monogamous, committed, or any other relationship word. In fact, he and Laney didn't really *have* a relationship. They had sex. Hot, rough, mind-blowing sex. He shouldn't want anything more. But he looked at her and he wasn't empty or emotionless. He was the *opposite*. She made him feel too goddamned much, and he'd picked a hell of a time to figure that out, too. Sex with a near-stranger was more his style, a meaningless hookup that meant he didn't have to worry about pleasing an exclusive lover.

He didn't want to have fantasy-suite date-night sex or whatever the reality TV shows were calling it these days. He just wanted… Laney. Wanted to hear the soft, whimpering noises she made, lose himself in her smile. *Danger.* He wasn't emotionally attached. He couldn't be.

"Maybe we could skip the fantasy stuff and just…"

"Have normal sex?"

"That, too," he said, knowing he sounded gruff. But damn, was he really going to use the words *making love*?

"You have a fantasy about doing it missionary style?" A smile curved her lips. Jesus. He needed to make a strategic retreat.

"What's wrong with making love face-to-face?" He rolled over, pinning her beneath him. Maybe he needed to be more *show* and less *tell*.

"Nothing." She curled her arms around his neck. "Step one? Accomplished."

"That way, you can tell me how I make you feel. What you enjoy and what you want more of."

"Uh-huh." She leaned up and brushed her mouth over his ear. "I feel like I'm melting."

Melting was good. He settled between her thighs as she wrapped her legs around his waist.

She wasn't done talking, though. "And do you whisper back?"

"I do. I've got lots of things to say to you."

"And do?" He wasn't sure which was better—the hopeful note in her voice or the way her fingers tightened on the back of his neck, pulling him closer until his lips grazed hers.

"Absolutely," he said and proceeded to show her.

13

GRAY WOKE UP at zero-dark-thirty as he always did, years of training kicking in. His side ached liked a bitch, and he had a cramp in his left shoulder because—*wait for it*—he'd apparently spent the night cradling Laney against his chest. She had one arm draped over him, the other smashed somewhere beneath the blanket. The ache in his shoulder wasn't the problem. Nope. The problem was the urge to do it again. Over and over, if he was being honest.

Which he'd been *last* night.

First about his upbringing, and then about his feelings. Memories came flooding back, of him telling her how special she was. Of how she made him feel. He'd all but spouted poetry, and he probably would have done *that*, too, if he'd known anything besides country music lyrics.

He stared at the window, but there were no answers there, either. The window provided a prime view of several overgrown palm trees. The screen had a hole, and the window itself was a liability, but he liked the fresh air, and he wasn't expecting snipers in the coconut palms. The bed was small and that was the only reason why he'd draped Laney on top of his chest like the best kind of blanket. Nope, no other reason at all.

He looked down at the woman in his arms. Laney's sleek hair wasn't so sleek. Brown curls stood up on one side, and she looked adorably disheveled. She was also naked and seemed extremely comfortable curled up against him. As if she belonged there. Which probably explained the feeling of panic that roiled through him.

The sensation was unpleasantly similar to one he'd enjoyed during BUD/S training, when his instructor had tied his hands behind his back and then Gray had voluntarily stepped into the training pool, hit the pool floor nine feet down, and bounced back to the surface. Could you drown-proof your emotions? Because this wasn't simply sex anymore. In fact, there was no *just sex* about it at all. He was on the bottom of the pool, in the deep end, and he wasn't bouncing back from this anytime soon.

Laney mumbled something in her sleep. He needed an exit plan. A do-over. Some sage advice.

Instead, he got a sharp knock on the door. Somehow he doubted it was room service. Laney immediately opened her eyes, shoving upright. He woofed out a breath, because she didn't pussyfoot around.

"Coming," she groaned, batting around the bed with her hand. He had no clue what she was looking for—pager, stethoscope, bone saw—but he was glad he didn't make a habit of sleeping with loaded weapons under his pillow. She was a hazard half-awake.

She paused. He knew the moment she realized she was naked, because the blush came back. "That wasn't my pager."

At least she'd had nonlethal intentions. The knock at the door was repeated.

"Stand down, Doctor." He dropped a kiss on her forehead and got out of bed. When he cracked the door, he found Levi standing in the hallway.

Levi eyed him. "R&R?"

"Off-limits."

Levi nodded. The man was already geared up. "Party time. We've got a helicopter incoming in thirty minutes."

"At the crack of dawn?" Who brought his girlfriend to a romantic island getaway before the sun even rose?

Levi grinned. "Marcos is an early riser. Or he hasn't been to bed yet. Possibly, he knows that the fewer people who see him arrive, the better. Ask him yourself when we bag him."

He nodded. "I'm ready to roll in two minutes."

Shutting the door, he started pulling on his clothes. "I have to go."

Lame. She wasn't deaf. She'd heard Levi.

"I'll go, too." She didn't seem upset, but he kept an eye on her as they got dressed.

Falling asleep with Laney had not been part of his plan. The sweet-whispers thing was fantasy material, sure, but this was real life. He'd intended to have sex with her, hold her some because he knew that mattered to her and then walk her back to her bungalow where she'd be safer. And, as an added bonus, returning her to her place would have avoided the whole awkward morning-after conundrum because, yeah...he felt naked and not because he was only half-dressed.

Last night he'd enjoyed the hardest, fiercest orgasm of his life, and she'd been right there with him. He was fine with that part of the night's agenda. But then he'd wrapped his arms around her. He'd held on and rubbed her back, and he might have…said things. Needy things along the lines of *You were fucking amazing* and *Thank you* and *I can't believe someone like you has time for someone like me.* And when she'd drifted off to sleep, he hadn't let go then, either. He'd held her and breathed her in, burying his face in her hair and pretending he'd never forget the apple scent of her shampoo or the way she curled a delicate foot around his leg. She was supposed to get up and go. And, if she didn't, he was supposed to pick her up and carry her back to her own bed. He could have done it, too.

But he hadn't.

He'd fallen asleep, still cuddling her, and now his entire team knew it. He never slept with his lovers. Sleeping was a private thing. It was one thing to strip down to his bare skin, and he'd never had a problem with serving up raw, gritty sex acts. Bluntly put, he had an expiration date. He wasn't a long-term guy, and sleeping together was the kind of thing a woman did with her keeper man. He'd touched Laney everywhere, put his fingers inside her body. He'd kissed her, caressed her, licked her from head to foot. Those things didn't bother him. The sleeping thing, however, was unnerving, and he felt out of control. Mission gone sideways, although not FUBAR. Just…uncharted waters. He grabbed a T-shirt while he thought that one over.

She ran her fingers through her hair, braiding it loosely. "You've got a thing."

Busted. He couldn't tell her the details, and that was just one more reason in the *con* column for having a relationship with a SEAL. He had to go, and he couldn't tell her where, why or even for how long.

"You okay walking back to your bungalow alone?" he said instead.

There was a pause as she fished for her sandals with her toes. "I think I can manage," she answered dryly.

"You can stay here if you prefer."

"Alone." Now she sounded put out.

He jammed his feet into his boots, bent over and started lacing. "Those are your only two options."

She sighed. "We need to work on our mornings after."

He didn't think they'd sucked so badly. "I'm not complaining."

"Because you're the one leaving to go to work."

"How did you think it would go?" Genuinely curious, he started grabbing weapons. He had a .40-caliber Glock model 17 with four magazines, a KA-BAR knife, and a Heckler & Koch MP-5 machine gun holstered to his thigh. He'd need to grab more multiple magazines for the machine gun, .40-caliber Teflon-coated hollowpoints designed to pierce any body armor, including the SEALs, because he didn't know how well prepared Marcos would be. She made a choked sound and he looked up. "What?"

"They let you bring all that stuff onto Fantasy Island?"

He snorted. "We didn't have to worry about the TSA. We rode a commercial airliner into our drop zone and then we bailed out."

The flight had taken off from Miami International looking like any tropics-bound jetliner, except the passengers had been almost exclusively male. Gray and his team had schlepped carry-ons full of jump gear, and the cargo hold didn't hold suitcases. They'd popped the door and jumped when they got near Fantasy Island. It wasn't a bad way to travel as long as you avoided the jet engines and timed the jump right.

"Right. I can see the 3-1-1 liquid rules didn't apply to you."

Jumping with sixty-five pounds of cargo, aiming for a quarter-mile stretch of sand? Yeah. TSA's rules had not applied in that situation. He rolled his shoulders, settling his harness in place. The chitchat thing was strange. Not strange bad, but completely unfamiliar. But he needed to get his head in the game and his ass into the hallway. It was showtime, not express-your-feelings time.

"You're injured," she reminded him. "Even you, Mr. Super SEAL, can't heal that quickly."

"It's just a scratch," he said gruffly.

"And you have a medical degree from the University of WebMD?" She yanked up the hem of his T-shirt. "Hold this."

Part of him wanted to push her away. He didn't take orders and he was out of time. But normal folks expressed concern when their loved ones were going away on a business trip. Or in deep shit. Or running the risk of dying. Yeah. He'd stick with the business trip analogy. So he stood there, holding up his shirt, while she reapplied a bandage, her movements quick and efficient as she taped the gauze in place. This mattered to her, so it was the least he could do.

"There." She stepped back and he dropped his shirt. "You'll do."

His body held no surprises. He'd been X-rayed, tested and poked to death before he'd been allowed to join a special warfare training compound as a SEAL trainee. After that, he'd trained, honed and disciplined that body. There was no one type of man who made it through

SEAL training. Big guys, little guys, it was all about the motivation and having the sheer determination and will. So he wasn't worried about the bullet. He knew what his body was capable of and he'd be fine.

Nope. The problem wasn't his body. It was his god-damn heart. He had something stuck in it, and he was pretty certain it was Laney.

She met his gaze. "Where is this going?"

They both knew he couldn't tell her the details. On the other hand, he didn't want her worrying—or trying to follow him. "The landing zone on the other side of the island. We have incoming."

She stared at him, the familiar pucker forming between her eyebrows. "This isn't about helicopters."

Right. She'd meant *them*.

"Never mind." Her sigh ruffled his hair, and he wanted to smooth away the frown, memorize the answer that would make her happy.

"Well, good luck…" Pausing, she tilted her face up to his. That was his cue, but he felt as if they were playing out another fantasy, one he hadn't been given the script to. How did civilians do this? Hand over a cup of coffee, plant a kiss on her lips and hightail it? Planning. He needed to plan more the next time.

When he *still* didn't say anything, because he was a dumbass, she hitched in a breath and stepped in closer, sliding her hands up his arms and over his shoulders. His arsenal had to be digging into her, but she didn't seem to mind. Laney was a good sport and practical to boot. God, he needed to go. To find some drug-runner ass to kick. But another part of him wanted to stay right here, with this woman.

"I need you to come back to me, okay?"

That had been the wrong thing to say. Fantasies were just that—fantasies.

She knew it even before Gray froze in the doorway. She needed a do-over, a list of witty things to say when your lover geared up and headed out on a secret military mission. "I don't go looking for trouble," he said, his voice low and gruff. "But I never walk away from a fight when it finds me. Some of us, we walk the wall holding our rifles, and we never pull the trigger, but me, I'm part of a unit where I'll aim and fire if that's what the mission requires. I think you should know that."

Gray bristled with weapons and camo, a look that was part sexy, part scary because this was no game. He was really going to go out there and, if he had guns, so would other people. Soldiers got hurt. She should know. She'd already sewn him up once. Stretching up on tiptoe, she pressed a kiss against his stubble-roughened cheek. The gesture was another inappropriate move, but she wanted the kiss for herself.

"Got it," she said.

This wasn't how she'd imagined their night ending. Although, really, what had she thought would happen? Pancakes at an all-night diner? A declaration of love? Pancakes were good and she'd bet the resort's restaurant would cook them, but he was her breakup man, her fun-times guy. She hadn't planned on keeping him, so it was good he was already on his way out the door.

GRAY AND LEVI lay on their stomachs in position on the western side of the road leading from the landing pad to the resort. Remy and Mason had the east side. A shooting pair was focused on the apex of the ambush. That gave them six shooters on this stretch of road. The rest of the second SEAL team had the backside of the landing pad covered. If the SEALs riding the jeeps couldn't disarm Marcos—and no one believed the man would come unarmed—and Marcos broke away, Gray, Levi and the others would provide crossfire in the kill zone. Taking their perp alive was the priority, but they'd take him down if it were the only option.

From his vantage point, Gray couldn't see the thatched-roof hut just down the jungle track that served as the resort's "airport." Everything there would seem normal, with no telltale clues that two teams of SEALs had replaced the usual staff. Two jeeps waited to meet the arriving guests, and Gray had SEALs in both vehicles, along with more SEALs dressed in the advance team's clothes. Marcos shouldn't realize anything had happened until he was boots down on the ground.

The jungle slowly woke up around them. Birds called back and forth over the whine of insects, and a male howler monkey vocalized in the distance. With his legs spread, Gray's boots touched Levi's. Even when the helicopter came into sight and they went silent, he wouldn't be alone. He'd be toe to heel and in constant communication even though moving wasn't an option. According to Ashley's inside source, Marcos planned to time his arrival for sunrise. That wasn't optimal flying time, but apparently, Marcos's girlfriend had declared it romantic and a symbol of new beginnings. He'd bet Marcos had loved that. If all went according to plan, she'd be pulled away from Marcos and out of any possible firefight. Gray didn't know how much she understood about Marcos's business dealings, but Uncle Sam had a list of questions with her name on it.

As if he'd read Gray's mind, Levi turned his head. "We need to discuss your dating strategies."

"Now?" It was still ten minutes until go-time. He listened, but couldn't hear the chopper's blades yet.

"You see a Starbucks where we can grab a coffee while we wait?" Levi's teeth were a slash of white in his face paint.

Gray shifted slowly on his belly, easing into a more comfortable position. The jungle floor was no Barcalounger. "If you want to try and have a heart-to-heart while we're setting up an ambush, be my guest."

"You can get up and leave. Not without blowing the mission." Satisfaction filled Levi's voice.

"Is this payback?" He racked his brain, but he couldn't remember tweaking Levi about his love life recently.

"Friendly advice." The other man eased up on his elbows and scanned the road.

"Since when do you play psychoanalyst?"

"Since you forced me to overhear your sweet goodbyes with Doctor Laney." Levi grimaced and sank back down, near invisible on the jungle floor. "Plus, I'm bored. Anyway, you need to work on both your delivery and your content."

"That was private." He'd hoped.

Levi grinned. "Don't be such a girl."

"I could quit," he warned. "Text Uncle Sam my resignation right now and walk away."

Levi snorted. "And Uncle Sam could take his own sweet time accepting your resignation. Remy's been waiting six months to hear back on his."

"I could shoot you. Solve my problem quicker."

"You like me." Levi grinned. "Besides, I'm going to hand you the keys to Laney's heart."

"We're not serious," he said. Which was a stupid thing to claim because if he knew one thing, it was that Laney confused the hell out of him. She was sweet and open and trusting. While he...was not.

Levi shook his head. "Keep telling yourself that."

"Shut up."

Of course Levi didn't. The man was unstoppable when he had something, and he only had about eight minutes to get it said before Marcos landed and they both got more than a little busy.

"She asked where you thought the two of you were going. That, my man, was the part where you should have told her that you were glad the two of you were having that conversation. If you're in a sharing mood, you tell her you're really interested in her. Bottom line, you let her know she's more than a convenient hookup."

"Noted." Was that a helicopter he heard? Action would be welcome because, damn it, he was sick and tired of lying here like a log with only Levi and his thoughts for company. He knew that this thing with Laney was more than sex, and it scared the hell out of him. Shooting something would be a welcome change of pace. And since he doubted Marcos would go down without some kind of fight, he estimated his wish would come true in approximately seven minutes.

The rhythmic *thwup-thwup* of an incoming helicopter interrupted Levi's answer, followed shortly thereafter by the sound of tires crunching over the dirt track. The first jeep came into focus: two bodyguards, the resort driver, Marcos and the girlfriend. The second jeep carried two more guards and a mountain of Coach luggage. He repositioned, sighting his rifle.

As soon as the first jeep crested the track, Levi lobbed

a flash bang into its path. There was a bright flash followed by a clap of sound. The grenade would disorient the jeep's occupants for a few seconds.

"Let's move." Surging to his feet, Gray ran for the lead jeep.

The SEAL in the driver's seat had hit the brakes hard. One of the guards had been thrown clear, and Gray signaled for Levi to take charge of him. The driver had gone for bodyguard number two.

"Manos arriba," Gray barked. *"Arrondilese."*

Anyone stupid enough to ignore the order and draw would be picked off by the sharpshooters up in the trees. The girlfriend turned out to be a shrieker, but Sam took care of that fast, wrestling her off the jeep and to the ground, one palm over her mouth.

Ramming his shoulder into Marcos, Gray secured the perp's handgun and tossed him onto the ground. The man fought like a son of a bitch, surging back onto his feet, and Gray had to hand it to him. The guy knew how to take care of himself. Maybe hand-to-hand was a required skill in the drug trade these days. One well-aimed punch to the jaw took Marcos down, however, and Gray zip tied the man's hands behind his back and patted him down for weapons.

Two guards down, Marcos and the girlfriend secured. Check, check and check. He swept the area, looking for potential issues. The other unit was all over the second jeep, but then gunfire erupted. Shit. Both the sharpshooters and Gray's team had silencers. Any noise had to be coming from the two bodyguards in the second vehicle.

"Report," he barked. Bullets sprayed the ground and then stopped.

Sam rose up from the other side of the second jeep. "We're clear, but we've got a problem."

Gray sprinted toward him. On the other side of the second jeep, Remy leaned heavily against the jeep's side, bleeding profusely.

14

GRAY SLIPPED THROUGH the darkness toward Laney's bungalow. Mission accomplished, bad guy in custody. Marcos would be on his way to the mainland and a US military prison within the hour. And Gray was confident that whatever intel the man had would eventually make its way to the right ears. Useful ears. Unfortunately, the mission hadn't gone entirely his unit's way. Right now one of his guys was possibly bleeding out, spending the last minutes of his life lying on the jungle floor some eight hundred miles from the Louisiana bayou where he'd been born and raised.

That wasn't happening on Gray's watch, not if he could help it. Which explained why he was inbound on Laney's bungalow, the jungle alive around him with early-morning wake-up noises, and worse, as the birds and the howler monkeys took notice of his presence. He'd abandoned the *covert* part of *covert op* in favor of a six-minute mile.

He sprinted up the path, hoping that any early-rising guests would write him off as a fanatic jogger. Unfortunately, time was not on his side. Laney's bungalow was on the resort's northern perimeter. Once again, he cursed the resort's owners for the pro-green stance that had banished golf carts and any other form of motorized transport from Fantasy Island. Bicycles were encouraged, but locked up overnight. By the time he'd picked the lock on the storage shed, he might as well have hoofed it on foot.

When he turned the corner, Laney's bungalow was dark, the curtains still drawn. He raced up the steps and swiped the keycard through the lock. Ashley had assured him the master card would open any door, and it appeared she'd been correct. The lock flickered green and he heard the door pop. He was in.

Stepping inside, he quietly closed the door behind him. Leaving the door open would invite questions if anyone passed by, and housekeeping would be starting soon. He looked toward the bed, hoping for movement. This wasn't the way he'd wanted to come home to her. Not that he'd thought about it or her during his mission. Not more than once or twice at any rate.

Then he saw her. Sprawled on top of the covers, she wore only a T-shirt and shorts, despite the fact that she'd once again air-conditioned the bungalow to roughly the inner temperature of an igloo. She'd foregone a ponytail, a red-letter day, and brown hair spilled over the pillow, clearly visible in the light from the bathroom. She hated the dark. She'd mentioned that once, sounding sheepish, and he'd thought it was cute. Unlike her, he loved the dark.

The even in and out of her breathing filled the room. God. She looked peaceful. Happy even. He hated like hell to wake her up, but Remy was out of time and she was his best chance at survival.

He crouched down beside the bed and placed one hand on her shoulder. The other he rested near her mouth. He couldn't risk a scream, but he didn't want to scare the crap out of her. It was bad enough he'd suddenly materialized in her room without an invite. He wouldn't make this worse for her if he could help it.

"Laney." He brushed his mouth over her ear. Okay. So the almost-kiss was for him. He suddenly understood that picture of the sailor kissing a random woman when he docked, sweeping her back and off her feet. He felt the same way when he saw Laney, as if he could laugh and jump into the bed and wrap himself around her. Kiss her some, love her lots.

No. That was the wrong word. He definitely didn't do *love*.

"I need a doctor," he said, more roughly than he'd intended.

She came awake in a rush and it was easy to imagine her as the attending doctor at a hospital, catching a catnap in an empty room. Waking up when the nurse came in or the pager went off. She woke up as if she expected it, as if she'd never quite allowed herself to relax completely.

"Gray?" His name, sleepy and soft.

"Yeah, sweetheart. It's me." He touched her cheek. The gesture was selfish, but he couldn't help himself. Teammates had used the words *big*, *mean* and *bastard* to describe Gray, and they weren't wrong. He certainly had no business inviting himself into her bedroom, no matter how welcome she'd made him before. The regret was a new emotion, regret for what he'd done, the women he'd slept with. Funny how sex had seemed to fill the empty hole inside him but now he felt emptier than ever.

"I hate to ask this." But he would.

"Okay," she said, sitting up and rubbing the sleep out of her eyes. Something flashed over her face. Hope? Anticipation? Hell if he knew, but one thing was certain. Whatever it was, he was going to disappoint her.

"I've got a man down and Sam's out of his league. I need you to take a look."

She stared at him for a moment. "Okay," she repeated. She swung her legs over the edge of the bed and stood up. From his position on the floor, he had an excellent view of her long, bare legs and tousled hair. Her T-shirt had rucked up around her middle while she slept, and she tugged it down absentmindedly.

"How bad is it?" She hurried over to the closet and rifled the contents, grabbing clothes and shoes.

Sam had coached him on what to say. "Gunshot wound with severe vascular trauma."

She cursed and dropped the clothes. Adrenaline hit him hard. Remy was in bad shape. He got that. But if he got her back quickly, maybe there was still hope. Her next words took it away.

"That's not good, Gray."

But Remy wasn't dead, which meant there was still some hope left. Ignoring her clothes, she yanked on socks and sneakers, pulling her hair back in a ponytail. He wanted to say thank you, to acknowledge what she was doing. She had his team's back, and she didn't know what was waiting out there for her.

"The threat's been neutralized," he said gruffly, in case she was worried. "I'm not taking you into a hot zone."

She nodded and turned to face him. "I know."

There was no way for her to know that.

"I know you," she continued. "If it was still danger-ous, you wouldn't put me in harm's way." The trust in her voice was a surprise. He didn't know when he'd earned that or what to make of it. He didn't have time to explore the unexpected feelings, however, because he had a man down. She was a doctor. He needed her. Right now, it was as simple as that.

She rushed for the door. "Let's hit the road. You may have to carry me back, but we can run until we get there."

LANEY CRUNCHED ALONG behind Gray. Or, more accu-rately, ran. Gray set a brutal pace, pushing for an eight-minute mile. He might run every day, but she'd been loading up on too many desserts. A stitch tore through her side, and breathing was its own challenge. Once again, she forced her breathing into an even rhythm, sucking air in a long, slow draw and releasing it the same way. Keep it even. Don't panic. So it was a killer pace. So she couldn't see where she was going. She could keep her eyes on Gray's back in front of her, leading the way. Except he bristled with weapons like some kind of le-thal hedgehog, and she kept remembering the way his paint-streaked face had risen over the edge of her bed.

Her first response had been to pull him in with her, wrap her arms and legs around him and hold him close. Relief followed by a chaser of disappointment, because he hadn't come back for *her*. He'd come for a doctor. At least he wasn't the injured SEAL this time. That was something.

The helicopter pad emerged out of the darkness, a barely illuminated concrete rectangle surrounded by jeeps and SEALs. Gray slowed to a fast walk and she almost crashed into him. He reached out a hand to steady her.

She surveyed the scene, looking for her patient. The SEALs were working in near dark and quiet. She supposed gunfire would have advertised their presence to the resort's remaining guests, but the only source of light were the landing pad's colored perimeter lights. It would be sunrise soon, though, and the sky above the jungle was lightening fast.

A number of SEALs—at least, she assumed they were SEALs when they ignored her and Gray—were clustered around a group of men and a single woman. Not wanting to know, she jerked her gaze away. Gray wouldn't tell her the details of his mission, but she knew the basics. These men were fighting to keep her safe. They were heroes, and she wasn't going to get in their way.

Gray guided her with a firm hand at the small of her back to the edge of the jungle. She could see Mason crouched on the ground, talking in a low voice on a radio. Sam was bent over a prone figure, his face intent on his task. That had to be her victim.

She dropped to the ground beside Sam. "Talk me through it. Give me the ABCs."

Sam nodded. "Airway's clear, respiratory rate is high, breathing shallow, but patient is breathing okay on his own."

The shallow part was cause for concern. She assessed her patient, wishing she had an emergency department at her fingertips. The man might be alert, but he was definitely showing signs of shock, from the quick, rapid breaths to the bluish tinge around his fingernails. She clasped his wrist, not liking the weak pulse. Issue number one was clear. He'd taken several rounds to the abdomen.

She looked over at Sam. "Significant intra-abdominal injury and penetrating abdominal trauma. We need immediate transport to a trauma facility."

Sam nodded and she did a further visual assessment. It wasn't looking good. Blood had soaked through the victim's clothing. His eyes remained open, though, and he seemed somewhat alert, biting into his fist either for self-control or in an attempt to stay silent.

"Did you move him here?"

Gray spoke from behind her. "Yes. He was hit halfway down the road to the resort."

"I need to know how much blood he's lost." That was probably a lost cause, but if Gray or one of the other SEALs could quantify how much blood her patient had lost, it would be helpful.

She listened while Sam finished running through the ABCs of triage, giving her an assessment of disability and exposure. Stripping the man down so she could examine him from head to toe was ideal, but this wasn't a good venue. The hospital could assess more closely.

"Have you checked his back?" It was highly likely they were dealing with more than one injury.

Sam nodded. "Clear. The main injury is to his abdomen."

She pressed her hand against the victim's shoulder, letting him know she was there. "We're going to take care of you."

She didn't recognize him and it didn't matter. This was someone's son, husband, Saturday-morning soccer date. Or he wasn't. It didn't matter. He was the guy she was going to save.

"Is it okay if I take a closer look?"

Her patient nodded then groaned.

Close range, she decided, although it was hard to tell in the near dark. "Give me a light," she snapped and someone did. Lifting the pads off his abdomen, she eased off on the direct pressure and got her first good look. No arterial pumping, thank God, but she definitely had a major vascular injury on her hands. Frankly, she was amazed he was still conscious. "How are you doing?"

His eyes fluttered closed. "I hope Uncle Sam bought trip insurance for my vacation."

She did, too. "You got a name for me, soldier?"

"Remy." He mumbled something else, but then he passed out.

"He needs surgery. Belize City is probably the closest facility." There was only so much she could do out here on an island. She needed a sonogram and an emergency department, an operating room and a full team.

Gray returned and crouched down beside her. "The medevac is inbound."

"ETA?" Remy was almost out of time.

"Two minutes. If I could get it here faster, I would." Team first. That truth was written all over his face.

When the chopper landed, Gray bent over Remy, shielding the man from the rotor wash blasting past the barrier of the jeep. Five minutes later Remy was on a stretcher, headed for the bird. She kept up the pressure on his abdomen, forcing the Medevac's personnel to lift around her.

"I'll ride with him," she said.

Gray hesitated, and she had no idea what was going through his head. Typical. She'd bet he was the kind of guy who stoically provided rank and number only in the hands of an enemy. "If I don't, he'll bleed out."

He nodded as if he'd come to some sort of decision—when *hello*, doctor here, she knew what she was doing—and cupped her elbows with his hands, lifting her with Remy and guiding her to a seat in the chopper.

She focused on Remy and keeping the vein pinched shut. This wasn't how she'd planned on finishing her vacation, but she was grateful she could help. Ashley would pack her suitcase and send it on, or the resort would do it. She'd need her passport and her purse at the very least, but these were people who made things happen. She'd be okay.

And, once she'd safely handed Remy off, Stockton waited for her. Stockton wasn't her first choice, or even her second, third or fourth, but she knew she was lucky to have a job. Better yet, she'd still be working as a trauma surgeon, which was one more thing to be thankful for. She'd ride with Remy to the closest hospital, hand him over to the resident surgeon there and then head back to real life. She'd be back in the chute, running an emergency department, before the end of the week.

Going back didn't worry her. Not anymore. Now she was worried about this desire she had to stay. Gray had been her fantasy, a sexy dream of a man, but now it was time to wake up. So what if this wasn't the way she'd planned their goodbye? She'd miss him, and not just in bed, although the hot sex was part of it. She'd miss the everyday, real Gray—his sweet tooth, the gleam he got in his eye when he thought she was being funny, the way he tackled life head-on and got the job done. He was the strong pair of arms holding her at night and the steady heartbeat beneath her cheek, an emotional anchor she hadn't realized she'd come to count on. Even more, she'd miss all the things she *hadn't* had a chance to learn about him yet and now never would.

But they wouldn't have worked together as a couple. She knew that, deep down. Maybe it came from being a fixer. She fixed people on her operating room table. Sometimes you couldn't fix people. Sometimes you had to let them go, and a relationship with Gray was a nonstarter. She didn't know how to hold on, and he didn't want to be a keeper. So that left them drifting apart.

Gray leaned in, curving one big, warm hand around her bare knee, and she realized that she was still in her sleep shorts and tank top. She could say something now. Ask him if it was just her, or if their vacation hookup had become something more than a fantasy. And yet she looked at him and the words died in her mouth. He was the SEAL team leader. Her everyday life had no place for him, any more than there was room for her in his. That wasn't a blame game, but it was unfixable. She had to let him go.

He looked at her, concern visible on his handsome face. "Are you going to be okay?"

No. She wasn't.

"I'm fine," she said instead. "If you could ask Ashley to send my things on to wherever we're taking Remy, that would be great."

"Will do." For a brief moment it looked as if he might say something, but the rotors picked up speed, drowning everything in a wash of sound, and it was time to go. Apparently, her last conversation with Gray would consist of her making arrangements to have clean undies sent after her.

He leaned in and tied her hair away from her face.

The strands were sticky with sweat and blood, and God knew she was a mess.

"All better," he said, but he was wrong. So wrong, but she had no idea how to tell him that. She mumbled her thanks as he popped a helmet on her head and buckled her in. Most medevac birds lacked basic safety equipment, but this one was obviously the exception. She told herself that was a good thing. Remy didn't need any more injuries, and getting back to her life in one piece was a good thing. Whenever she looked down, the blood streaking her forearms and legs was a visible reminder that life could be all too short.

"Was there something else you wanted to say?" *For instance, I want to see you again?* She had to yell the words in an undignified roar to be heard over the *whup-whup* of the rotors, but this wasn't how she'd imagined their relationship ending. Okay. She hadn't imagined that part at all—she'd been too stuck on the hot sex portion of the relationship agenda—but this was no Casablanca moment, either.

He shook his head and patted her on the shoulder. Then he buckled her in. "You take care."

As if she was a dog he'd ordered to *stay*? She opened her mouth but, really, she was out of words. And options. He backed away, swung out the door and disappeared. And…that was that. Vacation hookup sex? Done and done. Except she'd wanted a last kiss. And maybe some meaningful words to go with it. A phone number. *Anything.*

Fantasy Island fell away beneath them, a green jewel in the middle of the bright blue Caribbean sea. The weather had finally cleared, and pink-and-orange light shot over the ocean's surface. The helicopter banked steeply, heading west. The vacation and the fantasy were over.

She didn't want them to be.

Or she wanted Gray to be sitting here. Not where Remy was—God, not that—but headed somewhere with her. A scrap of pink fluttered in her peripheral vision. Gray had fastened her ponytail with one of the ties he'd used on her. They'd had crazy, hot, fan-fucking-tastic sex. She thought she'd been looking to get over her breakup with Harlan, but what she hadn't realized was that she she'd actually been looking for Gray. He was more than a fantasy lover.

He just wasn't *hers*.

Not anymore.

She turned her head, but Fantasy Island was gone, the ocean sliding away beneath the chopper. Tears prickled behind her eyes and she blinked them away.

She hadn't thought in terms of *forever* or *mine*, and now that it was too late? Yeah. She was all over that. There was something about him and, even when he'd been on the job and running a covert op, he'd made time for her. He'd shown her a side of herself she didn't know she'd even had. And she liked that new, bold Laney.

And she more than liked Gray.

She loved him.

15

THE BLACK HAWK swung out over the water and headed away. The wash from the rotors that had kicked up stray bits of sand faded, and the windy racket in the palm trees died down. Remy would get the help he needed, and that was what mattered.

Funny, though, how the chopper resembled any other chopper from the outside. The bird tilted, sun glinting off its side, and banked away from the island. The door was shut, so his chances of spotting Laney were slim, but Gray still watched the chopper go until it was a dot on the horizon. He'd helped her load up, had given her the green light to accompany Remy, but he hadn't really thought about what it would mean. She was gone.

Mason elbowed him. "You're going to ruin your eyes."

And that was why God made sunglasses. He thumbed his down over his eyes. "I suck at relationships."

Unfortunately, Mason didn't disagree. He turned to face the jungle, ready to beat feet. "Maybe you just need a dress rehearsal or some practice."

"Laney wasn't a rehearsal." He couldn't imagine feeling anything more, anything better, than what he felt when he was with her. And now she was miles away from him and getting farther every second. Yeah. He was brilliant. "She was the real deal."

"Did you tell her that?" Levi rocked back on his heels. He didn't seem surprised that they were still standing on the helicopter pad.

"If I had, do you think she'd be somewhere between here and Belize?"

"She's a doctor," Mason pointed out.

True. "I'd have her number. We'd have plans."

Instead, everything was over.

"Personally, I'm anti deep feelings." Levi shrugged. "I find sex-only keeps things simpler."

Mason ignored Levi. "So you'll work it out."

Right. How? "She's a doctor. She has a job. I'm a SEAL and *I* have a job."

The logistics were overwhelming, but it was easier to focus on the physical difficulties of getting together with Laney than on messy things like emotions.

Mason eyed him. "Are you really going to make me play therapist here?"

Gray flashed him the bird. "If you've got something to say, say it."

"Fine. You'll work it out. You go after her, you tell her about these feelings." Levi looked pained, but Mason kept right on talking. "And then you'll probably have to do some groveling."

"Lots of groveling," Levi added helpfully. "Fall on your knees and beg. There are other options after that, but it depends on how the groveling and begging was received."

"Hello. She's Belize-bound. I'm here. How am I supposed to find her?"

Levi gave him an incredulous look. "You've got government resources. Use them."

"Ashley's a mean hacker," Mason pointed out.

"Or just mean," Levi muttered.

"You're a SEAL. You don't quit. You finish the mission." Mason shrugged. "Blah blah blah."

It was the *blah blah blah* part that had him worried because, holy shit, he was mentally substituting three different words. *I love you.* Of course, those were words he should have used earlier, preferably before Laney had gotten on that chopper and out of Dodge. Instead, he'd pushed her away.

"Go after her," Mason said quietly. "See what happens."

He was going to have to do that. Find her, say the words *I love you* and see what happened. He might fall on his face, but he knew one thing. He didn't have the *potential* to fall in love with her—because he'd already fallen.

THE STOCKTON HOSPITAL actually wasn't bad. In the two weeks since she'd left Fantasy Island and landed here, Laney's new emergency room had received a decent number of cases, and she'd had two actual trauma cases to go with the small-city onslaught of uninsured people with flu and twisted ankles. Not that the trauma victims were happy about their role in her current state of mind, but she'd keep her thoughts to herself.

Bottom line? Her mom had done well by her. She'd pony up a *thank-you* during their next call.

Since tonight was slow and she had a double shift,

she'd commandeered an empty exam room for a catnap. Unfortunately, the bedding didn't come close to what she'd had on Fantasy Island. When she made head of ER, she'd order real pillows, not these wafer-thin excuses bulk-ordered from a medical supply catalog. Maybe some of those white duvet things, too. Sadly, bedding aside, sleep played coy. Maybe because every time she closed her eyes, she saw a certain unobtainable SEAL and her blood pressure shot up. And it wasn't as if she could take out a billboard ad: *Have you seen this undercover SEAL?*

That thought amused her for the next five minutes of her non-nap. Maybe she'd get a nice five-car pileup. Or an explosion. Okay, not really, but she needed something to do. Stockton was a pleasant enough city. She had a rented condo. With real estate prices down, the prudent thing to do would be to purchase. *After* she finished digging her credit card out from her Fantasy Island jaunt. All she had now were the bills and the fading tan lines.

And a few purloined souvenirs, including the mason jar on her desk that she'd filled with sand and shells. Bringing the stuff home probably violated all sorts of US custom rules, but bonus, because she'd ridden with Remy to the hospital in Belize City, her luggage had followed her *virgo intacta* and she hadn't been forced to prevaricate to a crusty border agent.

Her phone buzzed, signaling she had a text, and she fished it out of her pocket with a sigh. The number was unfamiliar, however, so it wasn't an urgent case.

Incoming.

Uh. Right.

Who is this?

The answer, when it came, was explanatory.

Our next round of margaritas are on me.

Ashley.

How did you get this number?

The door opened as she read Ashley's answer.

Go easy on him. He's flirting with the L word.

She stared at the text and then looked up. Gray stood there in the spill of light from the doorway. He was in faded blue jeans, a black T-shirt stretched tight over his chest beneath a battered leather jacket. If that wasn't hot enough, he wore motorcycle boots. Temporarily blinded by the sudden blast of light, she squinted at his face. A smile tugged at the corner of his mouth.

"Hi," he said.

LANEY BOLTED UPRIGHT, clutching the lapels of her white coat together. He'd caught her sleeping. The pillow on the gurney sported a dent from her head, and her face was flushed. She had a crease down her cheek from lying on her hand. He flicked on the light and watched her pull herself together, although that only made him want to muss her up. Get her hot and bothered until the only person she saw was him.

Although the *seeing* part of today's visit might not last long.

She shot off the hospital bed, and the nurse who'd accompanied him cleared her throat, but he was too distracted by the sight of Laney to notice anyone else. He was wheels-down on this mission.

"Can I buy you a drink?" When the nurse coughed, more loudly this time, he stepped inside the room and shut the door. He didn't need an audience for this. Laney folded her arms over her chest and watched him come. Hell. Was that a good sign? Bad?

She looked good, though. She wore a pair of green hospital scrubs beneath an open white lab coat that was askew from her catnap. She looked rumpled and sleepy and not totally in control, although she was getting there fast.

"What are you doing here?" She shot him a cautious look, but she had a smile on her face. A tentative and surprised smile, but it was still gorgeous.

"Looking for you." He didn't have to think about that. Instead, he strode over and dropped a kiss on her mouth as he pulled her toward him. Fourteen nights without Laney and he was still coming to terms with this desperate need he had to hold on to her. Her lips softened beneath his and that was a good sign.

The door popped open and Laney jerked backward. The gurney jerked with her, sheets crinkling, as she butt-planted.

"Sorry." The nurse's giggle sounded unrepentant. "Doctor Parker, I thought you might want to know that we're not expecting any patients for at least thirty minutes."

"Good to know," Laney muttered as the nurse retreated and closed the door.

When she didn't reach for him again, however, Gray

dropped down next to her on the bed. The place wasn't the sexy digs they'd shared on Fantasy Island, and he'd never liked hospitals. A visit meant that either he was out of commission or a buddy was.

"Sorry," he said, although he wasn't. A polite request to see Laney had been denied by the nurse. He'd been forced to resort to the truth: that he was here to grovel and beg. The nurse had liked that. And that was *after* he'd made it past the front desk in the ER. He'd made three-day treks across glaciers that were simpler than negotiating the hospital.

Laney looked at the closed door. "She's going to think we're having kinky sex in here."

She pressed her fingers against her forehead, stifling a yawn in her arm. She had shadows underneath her eyes.

"We already have," he pointed out. "Just not in here."

Although he'd be happy to help her with that fantasy, too.

"Hello. *She* doesn't know that. And, since being able to look my coworkers in the eye when I meet them in the break room is a good thing, I'd prefer to keep it that way."

Okay. Clearly, Laney had no intention of making anyone she worked with aware of her relationship with him. Great. That was a bad indicator of success.

"How's Remy?" She folded her hands in her lap and stared at him expectantly. Next question.

"He's going to be okay. He'll be spending the rest of the year rehabbing, but he'll be back."

She smiled. "I bet you miss him."

"Yeah, but injuries are part of being on the team. We'll keep his spot warm for him until he's ready to come back." *Damn.* He'd mentally rehearsed this. He was supposed to be convincing. Romantic. He was *not* supposed to list the reasons a SEAL was a bad long-term relationship prospect.

"I'm glad he'll make a full recovery." This time she gave him the polite smile of a stranger. She looked like a stranger, too, in her hospital scrubs, stethoscope hanging around her neck. She'd also looked happy enough to see him until he'd reminded her about the death and dying part of being a SEAL. *Go him.* Or maybe she'd really only been interested in a vacation fling, and his showing up here was awkward.

"Thanks," he said, because he was out of words. Ashley had offered to text him a script. He should have taken her up on it.

The silence stretched out awkwardly between them. Hell. Picking up her hand, he threaded his fingers through hers, rubbing at the muscles. He should have brought flowers. Picked out a card. Lingerie. *Something.* Because at least then they could fill up the empty spots talking about those things.

"Why are you here?" she blurted out.

"I…" *Say the words.* If he could charge an insurgent position, outnumbered and outgunned, he could do this. He could at least spit it out and hear what she had to say. Worst case, she shot him down and he slunk out that door. He'd already sussed out the exit points. There was a convenient stairwell out the door and to his left; he wouldn't have to do the walk of shame past the nurses' desk. "I missed you," he admitted.

Okay. That was closer to the truth.

"Really?" She sounded skeptical.

"You bet. The chopper evac with Remy—that wasn't

how I wanted things to end. Can I be honest?" What if she said no? Then what? His whole plan consisted of tracking her down and telling her that he loved her.

"I think we do honesty pretty well." She bumped his shoulder companionably with her own.

And that was his invitation to take the plunge. "I didn't want things to end at all. I was really hoping we'd spend the rest of your vacation together and, after that, that there would be a way for us to keep on seeing each other." He cleared his throat. "I know you've got your job here and I'm based out of Coronado, but at least we'd be in the same state. I just want to spend time with you, to figure out a way to make this work."

Next time he had to give a speech, he was writing crib notes. On his hand, on an index card, hell, he'd hire a skywriter if he had to. Because he was running dry and she was staring at his face, as if some invisible message was tattooed across his cheekbones. He just hoped it was a good message. An *I love you* message.

He sucked in a breath. He could do this. He'd rappelled out of helicopters into choppy waters, stormed enemy insurgents laying down automated rifle fire and aiming to kill. Telling the woman he loved the truth ought to be easy.

Nope. So the only easy day was yesterday.

She arched a brow. "What about the fantasies?"

He'd be happy to role-play every night if that was what she wanted. "If we get together, you should know I'll do whatever I can to make you happy in bed. Or on the beach, the back of my motorcycle or anywhere else you want. I'm aiming to make all your dreams come true."

She blushed. "That's not what I meant."

"Help me out here, then."

"I wasn't sure if what we had on the island was *only* a fantasy." She shrugged nonchalantly, but her fingers tightened on his, that familiar little pucker creasing her forehead. "And sometimes fantasies don't translate to real life. They're gorgeous dreams and fun and they have an expiration date."

He sure as hell didn't feel that way.

"I'm not going to lie. I loved every minute of our fantasy nights, and I'm going to do my best to convince you to pick out a new fantasy every week for the rest of our lives if you'll let me. But the bottom line is that I love you." Hooking a finger in her stethoscope, he tugged her closer. "You're my fantasy. You're the only woman I'm dreaming about. Where I was empty inside before, now I've got you. You're right there in my heart and I'd like to wake up with you every day for the rest of my life."

Her eyes teared up. He'd screwed up. No surprise there. But he was all in and he didn't have a fallback position.

"I've got something in my eye," she announced. "That's all." She dabbed at her eye with the corner of his T-shirt. The sheet on the gurney crackled loudly, and he'd bet the nurse who'd shown him in had her ear pressed against the door. At least he could make the show worthwhile. Rolling backward onto the bed, he pulled Laney over and on top of him.

"Hi," he said again, looking up at her.

A smile lit up her beautiful blue eyes. "You came all the way out here to tell me that?"

"Uh-huh. And to offer to buy you a drink."

"I'm working." She sounded disappointed.

"So I'll make suggestions and you can think about it."

She squeaked. Or maybe that was because she'd just hit his chest. "Okay."

"So." He tugged until she straddled him like a cowgirl. Yeah. He had plenty of fantasies about this position. He kept on pulling until her mouth was inches from his. "Can I buy you that drink?"

"How many drinks do I have to choose from?" Her lips twitched, but she tunneled her fingers through his hair, settling down on his chest as if she'd never left.

"I've got three," he said hoarsely. *Don't screw this up, soldier.* "A *Lover's Lemonade,* a *Blushing Bride* and a *Honey, I Do Martini.* It's your choice, but I'm hoping that this time we can do one of my fantasies."

"The bartender *is* pretty sexy. Keep talking. Tell me about this fantasy of yours."

"I'm fantasizing about happily-ever-after together." Time to put it all on the line. "We'll figure out the details but, when we're apart, I want to know I'll be coming home to you. I love you."

And...silence. She stared at him while he ran his hands up and down her arms. "I'm dying here. Please say something?"

She flattened her palms on his cheeks, cupping his face. "You said the *L* word."

"I like you, I lust for you. And, hell, yes, I love you. I'll read you every word in the dictionary if that's what you want."

"I love you, too."

"You do?" Because that was too good to be true. He'd been shooting for a chance to win her heart, but could the battle really be already won?

"Mmm-hmm," she said, leaning in to kiss him. "I didn't realize when I went to Fantasy Island that I had a chance at my own real-life lover and hero. I knew I had a chance at starting over, but you're someone special, Lieutenant Commander Gray Jackson, and I'm starting my own list just for you. *Lovable* is at the top, but I'm adding new words every day. *Lion-hearted, loyal, logical...*" She grinned at him. "Definitely *lickable*. I have big plans for us."

That worked.

"You're my fantasy, my everything," he promised.

"You give good fantasy," she whispered, her mouth meeting his.

"Real life's even better," he said and kissed her.

* * * * *

Ready for more of Anne Marsh's sexy SEALs?
Watch for her next title,
PLEASING HER SEAL,
coming January 2016,
only from Harlequin Blaze!

COMING NEXT MONTH FROM

Available October 20, 2015

#867 THE MIGHTY QUINNS: MAC
The Mighty Quinns
by Kate Hoffmann
Emma Bryant wants a passionate, no-strings affair, and she's found the perfect man to seduce—bad-boy pilot Luke MacKenzie. At least, he would be perfect...if he didn't suddenly want more from Emma than a casual fling.

#868 UNDER PRESSURE
SEALs of Fortune
by Kira Sinclair
Former Navy SEAL Asher Reynolds isn't afraid of anything—except being on camera. Too bad his best friend's little sister, Kennedy Duchane, is determined to have him star in a documentary...and in her sexiest fantasies!

#869 A WRONG BED CHRISTMAS
The Wrong Bed
by Kimberly Van Meter and Liz Talley
Two firefighters, two mix-ups, two happily-ever-afters? Celebrate the holidays with two scorching-hot Wrong Bed stories in one!

#870 A DANGEROUSLY SEXY CHRISTMAS
by Stefanie London
Max Ridgeway has sworn to protect Rose Lawson, even if she doesn't want him to. But the beautiful Rose is temptation personified, and Max walks a razor-thin line between keeping her safe and giving in to his desire...

YOU CAN FIND MORE INFORMATION ON UPCOMING HARLEQUIN® TITLES, FREE EXCERPTS AND MORE AT WWW.HARLEQUIN.COM.

HBCNM1015

REQUEST YOUR FREE BOOKS!
2 FREE NOVELS PLUS 2 FREE GIFTS!

HARLEQUIN®

Blaze

red-hot reads!

YES! Please send me 2 FREE Harlequin® Blaze® novels and my 2 FREE gifts (gifts are worth about $10). After receiving them, if I don't wish to receive any more books, I can return the shipping statement marked "cancel." If I don't cancel, I will receive 4 brand-new novels every month and be billed just $4.74 per book in the U.S. or $5.21 per book in Canada. That's a savings of at least 14% off the cover price. It's quite a bargain. Shipping and handling is just 50¢ per book in the U.S. and 75¢ per book in Canada.* I understand that accepting the 2 free books and gifts places me under no obligation to buy anything. I can always return a shipment and cancel at any time. Even if I never buy another book, the two free books and gifts are mine to keep forever.

150/350 HDN GH2D

Name	(PLEASE PRINT)	
Address		Apt. #
City	State/Prov.	Zip/Postal Code

Signature (if under 18, a parent or guardian must sign)

Mail to the **Reader Service:**
IN U.S.A.: P.O. Box 1867, Buffalo, NY 14240-1867
IN CANADA: P.O. Box 609, Fort Erie, Ontario L2A 5X3

Want to try two free books from another line?
Call 1-800-873-8635 or visit www.ReaderService.com.

* Terms and prices subject to change without notice. Prices do not include applicable taxes. Sales tax applicable in N.Y. Canadian residents will be charged applicable taxes. Offer not valid in Quebec. This offer is limited to one order per household. Not valid for current subscribers to Harlequin Blaze books. All orders subject to credit approval. Credit or debit balances in a customer's account(s) may be offset by any other outstanding balance owed by or to the customer. Please allow 4 to 6 weeks for delivery. Offer available while quantities last.

Your Privacy—The Reader Service is committed to protecting your privacy. Our Privacy Policy is available online at www.ReaderService.com or upon request from the Reader Service.

We make a portion of our mailing list available to reputable third parties that offer products we believe may interest you. If you prefer that we not exchange your name with third parties, or if you wish to clarify or modify your communication preferences, please visit us at www.ReaderService.com/consumerchoice or write to us at Reader Service Preference Service, P.O. Box 9062, Buffalo, NY 14240-9062. Include your complete name and address.

SPECIAL EXCERPT FROM

*Kennedy Duchane and Asher Reynolds have been
fighting their attraction for years. But when she has to
help him overcome stage fright, a little sexy distraction
may be just the ticket!*

*Read on for a sneak preview of
UNDER PRESSURE,
the final book in Kira Sinclair's sizzling trilogy
SEALS OF FORTUNE.*

The sweet scent of vanilla tickled Asher Reynolds's senses.

Cracking one eye open, he stared up at Kennedy Duchane
looming above him. Her thighs were spread on either side
of his hips.

"I could get used to waking up to this, Cupcake,"
he rumbled, threading his fingers through her hair and
pulling her closer.

Something soft and wet swept across his cheek.

"What the hell?"

She grinned wickedly, and for the first time he realized
she held something in her hand. A pale cupcake with a
thick swirl of bright pink frosting.

Eyeing it, he asked, "What is that?"

Her grin widened. "Payback."

Before he could even twitch, the thing was top-down
in his face. Kennedy smeared the sticky mess from his
forehead, down his nose and across his chin.

There was no question, he was under siege.

Asher grabbed her by the waist and flipped her onto her back. He wasn't about to make this easy.

With one hand, he captured her wrist, holding her arm above her head and immobilizing her weapon of choice.

She hadn't just brought one, but a full dozen of the sticky pink things.

Stretching out, he grabbed some ammunition of his own and struck. She yelped in surprise and tried to wiggle away. But he had her well and truly pinned.

"Nowhere to go, Sugar," he drawled.

Kennedy glared up. "Calling me Sugar is no better than calling me Cupcake, you Southern-fried Neanderthal."

Dipping his finger in the pink confection, Asher spread a smear across her collarbone.

"I only use nicknames with people I actually like," he murmured.

She squirmed. "Why Cupcake? It sounds so…empty-headed and pointless."

"Hardly." Pushing up onto his elbows, Asher gazed at her, his heart thumping erratically.

"*Cupcake* is the perfect description for you, Kennedy. The kind of treat you know you shouldn't want, but you can't seem to stop craving… Besides, I always knew you'd taste so damn sweet." He brushed his lips over her frosting-covered skin.

Don't miss
UNDER PRESSURE by Kira Sinclair
available November 2015 wherever
Harlequin® Blaze® books and ebooks are sold.

www.Harlequin.com

Copyright © 2015 by Kira Sinclair

HBEXP1015

Turn your love of reading into rewards you'll love with
Harlequin My Rewards

Join for FREE today at www.HarlequinMyRewards.com

Earn **FREE BOOKS** of your choice.

Experience **EXCLUSIVE OFFERS** and contests.

Enjoy **BOOK RECOMMENDATIONS** selected just for you.

PLUS! Sign up now and get **500** points right away!

Earn **FREE** REWARDS
HarlequinMyRewards.com
Join Today!

MYR16R

THE WORLD IS BETTER WITH

Romance

Harlequin has everything from contemporary, passionate and heartwarming to suspenseful and inspirational stories.

Whatever your mood, we have a romance just for you!

Connect with us to find your next great read, special offers and more.

 /HarlequinBooks

@HarlequinBooks

www.HarlequinBlog.com

www.Harlequin.com/Newsletters

HARLEQUIN®

A *Romance* FOR EVERY MOOD™

www.Harlequin.com

SERIESHALOAD2015